MYTHS OF THE WORLD

DEITIES AND DEMONS OF THE FAR EAST

MYTHS OF THE WORLD

DEITIES AND DEMONS OF THE FAR EAST

BRIAN P. KATZ

MetroBooks

MetroBooks

AN IMPRINT OF FRIEDMAN/FAIRFAX PUBLISHERS

©1995 by Michael Friedman Publishing Group, Inc.

Library of Congress Cataloging-in-Publication Data

Katz, Brian P., date–

   Deities and demons of the Far East / Brian P. Katz.

     p. cm. — (Myths of the world)

   Includes bibliographical references and index.

   ISBN 1-56799-091-6

   1. Mythology, Asian. 2. Gods, Indic. 3. Gods, Chinese.

4. Gods, Japanese. I. Title. II. Series.

BL1055.K38 1995

291.1'3'095—dc20   94-14613

                                       CIP

Editor: Nathaniel Marunas

Art Director: Jeff Batzli

Designer: Susan E. Livingston

Layout: Lynne Yeamans

Photography Editors: Susan Mettler and Wendy Missan

Color separations by HBM Print Pte. Ltd.

Printed in China by Leefung-Asco Printers Ltd.

For bulk purchases and special sales, please contact:

Friedman/Fairfax Publishers

Attention: Sales Department

15 West 26th Street

New York, NY 10010

212/685-6610 FAX 212/685-1307

DEDICATION

To Linda, Maria, and Craig.

ACKNOWLEDGMENTS

Special thanks to Sharyn Rosart, Lynne Yeamans, Nathaniel Marunas, and all of the other people whose hard work made this book possible.

CONTENTS

INDIAN
MYTHOLOGY

etween the years 1500 and 1200 B.C. the Indus valley was invaded from

the northwest by Indo-Aryan tribes. These invaders brought with them a

number of sophisticated texts, called *Vedas*. The Vedas were collections of

works that ranged over such subjects as theology, social institutions, legal

systems, ethics, cosmology, philosophy, and science. The most important of the

Vedas is the *Rig Veda*, compiled around 1000 B.C. and written in an archaic form

of Sanskrit. The *Rig Veda* is the oldest Vedic work and the basis for much

**Vishnu, one of the most important Hindu
deities, is depicted with his wife Lakshmi in
this magnificent eighteenth-century painting
riding the great sunbird Garuda.**

Hindu thought. In fact, although Hinduism remains a religion with no standardized form of worship, the *Rig Veda* is regarded as an authoritative text that is divine in origin.

Over time, the diverse stock of information contained in the Vedas was woven into the fabric of Indian life. Sometimes Vedas were adopted wholesale and sometimes changed and incorporated into the belief systems of the peoples of the Indus valley that already existed. Gradually, the Vedic influence was spread throughout the region, generally in the custody of the wealthy and learned class of men called *Brahmans*. As a result, Hinduism is sometimes referred to as Brahmanism. But there are a multitude of other forms of Hinduism as well, sometimes referred to as "village" Hinduism. These alternate forms of Hinduism are more firmly rooted in the pre-Vedic history of the Indus valley, and therefore make reference to many ancient and regional mystical beliefs and mythologies. One indication of the profound and lasting nature of Hinduism in general is the fact that the many different forms of Hinduism—from the animist to the monist—coexist peacefully in India.

Although the *Rig Veda* is the oldest accepted sacred work, Hindu mythology and theology are mostly derived from the Sanskrit masterpieces the *Mahabharata* and the *Ramayana*. These epics, which were developed gradually from around 400 B.C. to A.D. 400, relate the exploits of many deities, especially Brahma and his two main avatars, Vishnu and Shiva. Another important source for Hindu mystical beliefs and mythology is the *Puranas*, which are later Sanskrit treatises that deal with legends, religious practices, holy places, and so on.

The central Hindu deity is Brahma, the god of creation and birth. Brahma's two godly avatars—Vishnu, the god of preservation, and Shiva, the god of destruction—round out what is known as the Hindu trinity (called the *trimurti*). This triad dealt with the salvation of the human soul.

Hindu worship incorporates a fundamental belief in reincarnation. Brahma created a universe that functioned in continuous cycles. Everything, even the gods, is believed to be subject to this cyclical pattern.

The early Hindus also developed a rigid caste system, which was derived in part from the concept of reincarnation. It was believed that man was born to fulfill certain predestined positions in society; he had specific duties to perform. According to the mythology, the first members of these castes originated from Brahma's own body. Brahmans and *Kshatriyas* were the top two castes. The Brahmans were the priests and teachers. They spoke and listened to the gods and performed

This eighteenth-century miniature, which is housed in the National Museum in New Delhi, depicts a scene from the *Bhagavata Purana*. Brahma is shown hiding Krishna's herd of cattle.

religious acts and sacrifices. Kshatriyas were usually members of the royal families, the ruling class, and were trained to be warriors. Their duty was to protect the people by using their military powers justly and wisely. The third caste, *Vaisyas*, comprised the merchants and farmers. The members of the fourth and lowest caste, *Sudras*, were born to serve the other castes. Aside from this strict system of hierarchy, there were those known as the Untouchables. These people carried out the tasks that were considered unclean. They were the hunters, fishermen, and builders, as well as the undertakers, who dealt with the cremation of corpses. (Mahatma Gandhi, the visionary civil rights leader, abolished the connotation of "untouchability" in the Constitution of India, written in 1950.)

According to the law of reincarnation, the manner in which one conducts one's life determines whether one rises or falls in the caste system when reborn. (It was believed that one was reincarnated approximately 82,000 times.) Someone who leads a virtuous life may eventually become a Brahman. Finally, the virtuous Brahman will be released from the cycle of earthly life and ushered into the heavenly world of eternal peace and knowledge known as *Brahmalok*, or "the domain of Brahma." On the Hindu map, Brahmalok was believed to exist at the apex of Mount Meru, north of the Himalayas.

The early Hindus believed that India was a universe unto itself, that its physical being was shaped and controlled by the gods. Because of this perspective, the world at large was considered to be an illusion that had been created by the gods. Accordingly, there were many mythological lands such as Brahmalok. For example, below the surface of India was a hell, called *Patala*, ruled by Yama, the king of the dead, and populated by the serpentine Nagas. By contrast, there also existed a paradise, *Vaikuntha*, that was the traditional dwelling place of Krishna. There were also many other realms that were associated with the gods.

Although in practice traditional Hindu rituals and legends are passed on from one generation to the next, the roots of India's rich mythological and religious heritage are to be found in the ancient Sanskrit texts. The *Rig Veda*, a composite of 1,028 hymns, contains tales of the elemental Vedic gods, including the three chief deities—Indra, Vivasvat, and Agni—and many other inferior gods. Indra, the king of the gods, was subject only to Brahma. Storms, thunder, lightning, and rain were at Indra's command. Vivasvat, the god of the sun, rode throughout the day sky in a shimmering chariot of gold drawn by seven ruddy horses. Agni, god of fire, was the mediator between the gods and humankind.

The Puranas were sacred poems that described the lives and exploits of the gods. For the most part, these texts contained stories told in verse, each section titled with the name of the god or avatar in question. In later times, *Tantras*, also in verse form, were written. The Tantras were religious poems that

This rendering of an episode from the *Bhagavata Purana*, sacred Sanskrit poems (the most important of which were written during the period between A.D. 300 and 1200), depicts Krishna during the "hour of cowdust." The painting is part of the considerable collection of Hindu art at the National Museum in New Delhi.

supplemented the older Puranas and instructed worshipers in how to perform modern ceremonies. The Tantras were written around the Middle Ages, when worship of the mother goddess Devi (Devi was the personification of the union of Shiva and his wife) increased. The "Devi-Mahatmya" was the Sanskrit poem written in her honor.

One of the greatest Sanskrit epics, and the longest single poem in world literature, is the *Mahabharata*. This eighteen-book work is the foundation of Hindu mythology and the major source of knowledge of classical Indian civilization. The *Mahabharata* contains approximately 200,000 lines compiled by many authors over hundreds of years. The

great text deals primarily with dynastic struggle and civil war, and recounts stories about mystical events and great battles. It includes the *Bhagavad-Gita*, or "Song of God," which is the most widely read and studied gospel in Hindu ritual. The *Mahabharata* also has a firm moral and philosophical base that dictates many religious and political laws.

The *Ramayana*, of epic size (but much smaller than the *Mahabharata)*, was composed by the master poet Valmiki. It tells the story of Rama, the seventh incarnation of Vishnu.

The religious and philosophical tracts known as the *Upanishads* are yet another source of Indian thought. Composed by various authors beginning in the seventh century B.C., the Upanishads are prose treatises that deal with (among other issues) the individual's soul (*atman*) and its relationship with the collective universal soul (*brahman*).

There are many other sources for the rich mythological and religious traditions of India, not the least of which is the living body of lore passed on from one generation to the next. The result of having so many sources—not to mention the many sects—is that there are innumerable variations of the same stories. The canon is rife with conflicting details, which serves only to enrich further a stock of tales that, after all, features many entities whose natures likewise encompass certain polarities (Shiva, for instance, is known as both creator and destroyer).

The philosophies of Buddhism and Jainism also contributed to and were influenced by Hinduism. Although both Buddhism and Jainism are atheistic at their cores, and embrace all people despite their castes, they nonetheless borrow from the vast palette of Hindu mythology to paint metaphorical and allegorical tales. Similarly, many of the tenets of Buddhism and Jainism (e.g., purification through leading a "good" life) are expressed in ancient Hindu texts and in the living religion.

Although India has remained mostly Hindu, around A.D. 600 the Islamic faith began to take hold. The regions known as Pakistan and Bangladesh separated from India because Islam (which is monotheistic) could not coexist with Hinduism (which is polytheistic), Buddhism, or Jainism.

OPPOSITE: This scene from the *Ramayana*, a 50,000-line poem about Vishnu's most popular avatar, Rama Chandra, depicts Rama, Lakshmana, and Visvamitra. Rendered in 1750, this painting is in the National Museum in New Delhi.

This sandstone carving of the Hindu triad (called the *trimurti*) depicts Shiva, Vishnu, and Brahma. It is part of the Temple of Shiva, on the island Elephanta, and dates from the seventh or eighth century A.D.

THE
SUPREME GODS

BRAHMA

Brahma, being one with Vishnu and Shiva, represented the creative force. According to legend, Brahma was born from the seed of his will. He was the primeval essence, the collective soul of the universe and the personification of everything in the universe. Brahma created the first egg, *hiranyagarbha*, the first object of creation and life. Having emerged from the egg without cracking it, Brahma, now physical, divided the egg. One quarter became man and one quarter became woman. A third piece became heaven and the fourth became earth. His first male incarnation was known as Purusha, the cosmic man, and his first female incarnation was Prakriti, nature. (According to other versions, Brahma himself split into a female and a male who together created the earth's people.)

In the continuous cycle, when Brahma breathed out (*sa*) the universe was created; when Brahma breathed in (*ham*), the universe was destroyed. Between breaths, the world existed for two billion years, a cycle within the cycle. After souls were reborn 82,000 times they entered an exalted state, where they received eternal wisdom and knowledge.

Brahma had four faces (a fifth was burned off by Shiva when Brahma spoke in a condescending manner to him). Brahma is depicted carrying in his four arms a vase, a bow, a rosary for prayer, and a copy of the *Rig Veda*. His wife was Sarasvati, also called Brahmi, the goddess of learning and music. Brahma was responsible for creating the elements—sun, moon, wind, water, and fire—and the gods who rule them.

VISHNU

Vishnu was the preserver, the restorer, and god of the sun. He may have been the most important figure in Hindu mythology. Many of Vishnu's followers claim that it was he who created the universe and not Brahma. (Although it may seem irrelevant whether the universe was created by Brahma or one of his incarnations, it is not: Hindu deities, despite the fact that they are all avatars [to some degree] of Brahma, are distinct entities, each capable of independent and even conflicting activity. Furthermore, different sects of worshipers attribute certain actions [like the creation of the universe] to the deity they favor.)

Of course, Brahma and Vishnu are also very closely linked—they are both part of *sat*, "that which is." Along with Shiva, they comprised the *trimurti* (the "three in one"); this triumvirate is responsible for creating the world. The prefix *vish* means "to pervade." His pervading powers have been recognized in each of his ten incarnations, which were usually in human or animal form. In some incarnations he was born from woman, while in others he arose by supernatural means. The avatars of Vishnu always appeared in the world to right wrongs and to save humanity from disaster.

Depictions of Vishnu often show him with blue skin, holding in his four hands a conch, a discus, a club, and a lotus. He rode the great sunbird, Garuda, who was also his trusted messenger.

As Matsya, his first incarnation, Vishnu took the form of a fish to save man from a deluge. As Kurma, his second incarnation, he took the form of a turtle and assisted in the churning of the ocean (from which activity several divine beings, not to mention an ambrosia of immortality, arose). In the form of a boar, Varaha, he again saved earth from a devastating flood. Narasimha, his fourth avatar, was half man and half lion. In this mythical form, Vishnu fought and defeated Hiranyakashipu, a demon-king strong enough to force Indra, the sky god, from his throne.

As Vamana, his fifth incarnation, Vishnu assumed the guise of a dwarf. His task was to regain control over the three worlds that were then ruled by the demon-king Bali. One day when Bali was offering a sacrifice, Vamana—also a Brahman priest—asked the demon-king for a boon.

"I ask you for a little patch of earth, as much as I can measure with three of my strides."

Bali agreed. The dwarf then grew into a cosmic giant and in two strides crossed the universe. With the third stride he stepped on the demon's head, defeating him. Not being a vengeful God, Vishnu banished the demon to rule a part of Patala.

In his sixth incarnation, Vishnu took the form of a Brahman, Parashu-Rama, who was both a holy man and a warrior. He came to earth, on the gods' behalf, to lessen the power of the Kshatriyas, the ruling class. He used his advanced knowledge of weaponry and his supreme mind to complete his task.

In the epic *Rama-yana*, Vishnu was incarnated as Rama Chandra, the son of King Dasa-ratha of Oudh, Sri Lanka. King Dasa-ratha was very devoted to Brahma and had acquired extraordi-

This exquisite eighth-century bronze statue of Vishnu shows the deity holding various sacred items and making a gesture of benediction with one of his right hands.

nary supernatural powers. The gods felt that the king had too much power and they appealed to Vishnu for help. Vishnu, as always, heeded the words of the gods and appeared before the king bearing a gift: a pot of nectar for the king's wives to drink. Dasa-ratha gave half the drink to his wife Kausalya, and she gave birth to Rama Chandra, who had half the divine essence of Vishnu. A quarter of the nectar was given to the king's second wife, Kaikey, and she gave birth to Rama's brother Bharata. Finally, the last quarter of the nectar was given to his wife Su-mitra, who gave birth to Lakshmana and Batru-ghna. Each of these children was instilled with some portion of Vishnu's essence and thus each was more powerful than the king.

Sage Visvamitra took Rama, at this point a young man, to perform two tasks. The first was to defeat a female demon who had been plaguing the countryside. For the second, Vishvamitra brought Rama to the court of Janaka, king of Videha. Rama instantly fell in love with the king's daughter, Sita. The king had decided that he would marry off his daughter to the winner of a contest of strength. The king had a sacred bow that belonged to Shiva. Offering up the bow to the contestants, the king announced that the man who could bend the bow would win his daughter's hand.

Not surprisingly, none of the suitors could bend the bow except for Rama, who not only bent it but broke it in half. Rama and Sita were married, and were very happy until Sita was abducted by Ravana, the most powerful demon in the universe. Rama, along with his faithful brother Lakshmana and the resourceful monkey god, Hanuman, relentlessly pursued his wife's captor. Many heroic adventures ensued until Rama was finally reunited with his wife.

ABOVE: Hanuman, the monkey god, was one of the more popular avatars of Vishnu. In the *Ramayana*, Hanuman helps Rama Chandra rescue Sita, Rama's wife, from the demon Ravana, who had abducted her to Ceylon.

RIGHT: An illustration from a scene in the *Bhagavata Purana*, this seventeenth-century miniature from the Court of Malwa shows Hanuman aiding Brahma in one of the supreme deity's adventures.

Whenever Vishnu was incarnated on earth, he was always reunited with his heavenly wife, Lakshmi. In the story from the *Ramayana*, Lakshmi was Sita. Together, Vishnu and Lakshmi represent the ideal marriage of one man to one woman.

The eighth and most popular incarnation of Vishnu was Krishna, the hero of the *Mahabharata* (and more notably the *Bhagavad-Gita*, which attests to his divinity). Krishna was born the eighth child of Devaki, wife of Vasudeva. Devaki had been impris-

oned by the powerful demon-king Kansa because it had been foretold that a son born to
Devaki would defeat the evil ruler. When
Krishna was born, Vasudeva smuggled the infant out with Vishnu's help. To conceal
Krishna's identity from the horrible Kansa,
Vasudeva exchanged babies with Yasoda, a
country woman who had given birth at the
same time as Devaki had. When Kansa found
that Krishna had survived, he sent six demons
to find and kill the child. Every one of these
dark minions failed in the task.

As Krishna grew into a man, he had many
adventures and destroyed many demons, but
one of the most important stories associated
with this incarnation of Vishnu was the tale
of the Gopis. Krishna was a gifted flute player,

and every time he began to play, the Gopis
(the cowherds' wives) dropped their work and
came running. For as long as he played, the
women would dance. Some believed that

Many cosmologies purport that the universe began as an egg, usually the divine creation of one of the members of the *trimurti* (depending on the particular sect). This arresting nineteenth-century painting, which is part of the collection at the Victoria and Albert Museum, shows Krishna in cosmic form, embodying the substance of the universe.

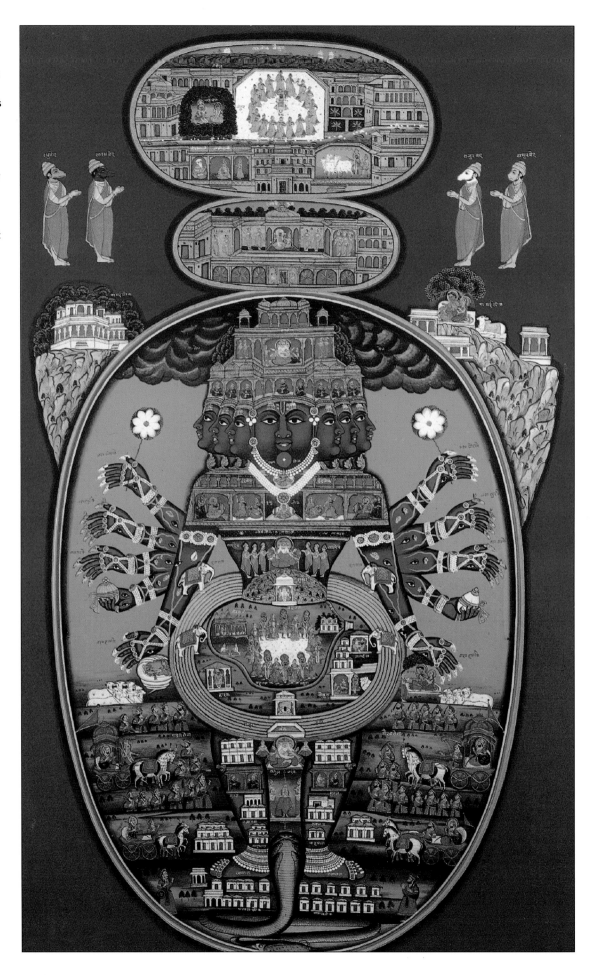

many orgiastic affairs occurred between the god and these married women, but others believed it was a very innocent—and indeed, symbolic—association. In fact, the relationship Krishna had with the Gopis is sometimes thought to be representative in Hinduism of the soul's relationship to the divine. By playing the flute, Krishna expressed his divinity. The women, in turn, expressed their selfless devotion (one of the two paths, in addition to self-knowledge, to self-realization) by dropping whatever they were doing and dancing to the music, which was an extension of the god. Appropriately, Krishna the demon-slayer is also the god of dance and music.

According to the beliefs of both Hinduism and Buddhism the ninth incarnation of Vishnu was the sage Buddha. The tenth and final avatar of Vishnu is Kalki. This, the final appearance of Vishnu during this cycle of the universe, has yet to come, but when this avatar arises he will appear in the form of a white horse.

SHIVA

Shiva, the third god of the *trimurti*, was the god of destruction. According to many beliefs he was also the god of the moon and the Himalayas. Shiva is often depicted (encircled by flames representing his divine powers) dancing the cosmic dance, moving to the rhythm of the universe. He is portrayed with blue skin (like his counterpart Vishnu), four arms, and four faces with three eyes each. The third eye, located in the middle of each forehead, possessed the supernatural power both to destroy and create. He wore the fur of a tiger and a scarf of snakeskin.

Shiva sat alone on the top of Mount Kailasa in the Himalayas, contemplating and meditating. Shiva was an ascetic and the god of the yogis (religious men who practice the power of mind over body). He was also known as Rudra, the howling one, the god of storms.

Rudra was the Vedic antecedent to Shiva, whose identity is intertwined with that of his Vedic forerunner.

The golden lines that radiated from Shiva's third eye symbolize destruction—not complete annihilation, but a waning, such as the end of the day or the coming of autumn—death for the sake of rebirth. Once, Shiva's wife Shakti (or Parvati) playfully covered his eyes. Everything in the universe went black, like a void. He opened his third eye, and order returned.

This painting, which was completed between 1760 and 1770, shows Shiva and Krishna attended by a bull, a tiger, and jackals. It is also housed in the Victoria and Albert Museum.

FAR LEFT: Bordering on Pakistan, the Rajasthan region of India is the home of many famous Hindu temples of worship. This beautiful and isolated temple is in the middle of Holy Lake.

LEFT: This stone lingam (a stylized phallic symbol associated with Shiva) illustrates the masculine principle of the universe. The female parallel of this type of representation is called a *yoni*.

Besides being the god of destruction, Shiva was also the god of the forest, the god of hunting and fishing, and therefore ruler of the Untouchables.

Shiva and his wife, Parvati, symbolize the ideal union—he is meditative, she is creative. They are two in one, calm and chaos, like life itself. Parvati's creative powers are evident in the tale of Ganesha, her son.

Once, when Shiva went away, Parvati created a boy from clay because she was lonely. She ordered him to stand guard while she bathed. It was at this time that Shiva returned home. He went to see his wife but was stopped by the boy. Enraged, Shiva cut the boy's head off. Parvati was stricken with grief. Upon seeing his wife weep, Shiva sent out his beasts to find a head that could replace the missing one. They came back with the head of a young elephant. He put the new head onto the boy's body and presented the ele-

phant-headed boy to his wife. She was overjoyed. The boy became Shiva's son. In Hindu mythology, the elephant was a character of great wisdom and knowledge. Ganesha became the god of wisdom.

One of the best-known tales about Shiva is also one of the creation myths. Meeting upon a sacred mountain, the gods decided to churn the ocean in order to refine from it the ambrosia of immortality. At this time the demons and gods were not yet enemies, so they worked together to stir up the ocean using a giant turtle mounted on the tip of an uprooted mountain. They spun this gargantuan churning device by using the enormous serpent Vasuki as the spinning cord. Various divine objects and entities were generated by this activity, as were many features of the world. Finally, the ambrosia was created, at which point Vasuki began to suffer from all the wear on his body, spewing poison everywhere from his one thousand mouths. Implored by Vishnu to save the universe, Shiva took the poison into his throat, which consequently turned blue. (The gods kept the ambrosia, which infuriated the demons, giv-

ing rise to an immense battle and the undying conflict between god and demon.) Because of his swallowing the poison, Shiva is sometimes known as Nilakantha, "blue throat." Shiva was also the patron of the demons.

OTHER HINDU GODS

There are many other deities in the Hindu pantheon, some of whom were native to the Indus valley and some of whom arrived with the Aryan invaders; many of course became composites of the indigenous and the foreign traditions. These gods were, like the universe, subject to the eternal cycle. They died and were reborn with the universe. They were seen as part of creation, part of the universe, but not creators themselves. Below are described several of the most important remaining Hindu gods and goddesses.

INDRA

Indra was the supreme Vedic god, and tales about him fill the pages of the *Rig Veda*. He was the king of the gods and the most powerful of the three primary elemental deities. He controlled the

RIGHT: Indra, the god
of storms, was one of
the three elemental
Vedic deities. He is
depicted here
carrying assorted
sacred objects and
riding an elephant,
symbol of his wisdom.

rains and storms, dispensing them according
to his whim. The lightning bolt was his
weapon. He rode an elephant, a symbol of his
wisdom and knowledge. His skin shone gold
and his huge arms encompassed the skies.
When Indra became the king of gods he created a heavenly domain known as Svarga.

Indra was the son of Dyaus-Pitri (Sky
Father) and Prithvi-Matri (Earth Mother).
Dyaus-Pitri and Prithvi-Matri were the parents
of all the older Vedic gods as well as of the first
humans. In Greek mythology, Indra's counterpart is Zeus. Both Indra and Zeus were the
progeny of a union between earth and sky.

Indra's wife was Indrani, the goddess of
the sky. Although he had many illicit affairs,
Indra shared his rule only with Indrani. One
of Indra's most noted love affairs was with
sage Gautama's daughter Ahalya. Indra, who
had the power to change into any form, transformed himself into the likeness of the sage

and seduced the all-too-willing Ahalya. Gautama caught the god as the latter was sneaking away after the tryst. The sage was so enraged with Indra for using his daughter that he visited a curse of impotence upon the god. As soon as the words of the curse were spoken, Indra's testicles dropped off and fell to the ground. Terrified, Indras asked his fellow deities to help him restore his virility. The gods replaced Indra's departed privates with the testicles of a ram.

Vritra (or Ahi), the serpent of drought, was Indra's archenemy. The two battled long and hard (and often), but Indra was always victorious (often winning battles in underhanded fashion). According to the *Rig Veda*, many other fights ensued between Indra and other demons bent on destroying the earth and the rule of the gods. These fights were symbolic of the eternal conflict between good and evil. The defeat of Vritra by Indra is one of the central episodes of the *Rig Veda*.

AGNI

Indra's brother, Agni, the god of fire, was the second of the three chief Vedic gods. He was omnipresent. A friend of humankind, Agni was the mediator be-

Agni, the Vedic god of fire and Indra's brother, was another of the elemental gods. It is believed that Agni is invoked every time a fire is lit, making him the overseer of many rites.

tween human and god. Agni had red skin, with two faces and seven tongues. His mount was a ram, another symbol of fire.

As the god of fire, Agni was essential to the practice of ritual sacrifice. When an offering was made to the gods, Agni, with all seven of his tongues, would lick the butter from the altar and then bring the essence of the burnt sacrifice to the heavens. All altars honoring the fire god were built to face the southeast, the direction of the sunrise, which was associated with Agni.

Agni created fire for cooking and for clearing the fields for farming. As the god of purification, he was responsible for cleansing corpses on the funeral pyre and taking their souls to heaven. He also united the bride and groom in the Hindu marriage ceremony when they encircled the sacred flame seven times. All uses of fire, beneficial or destructive, were associated with Agni.

The *Rig Veda* cites Agni as the father of Skanda, the general of the god's armies. In later Hindu myths, especially those related in the Puranas, Skanda is the son of Shiva.

VIVASVAT

Vivasvat, the third chief Vedic deity, was the god of the sun. Although many gods were associated with the sun (including Vivasvat's brother Agni, whose fire made up the sun, and the great Vishnu), Vivasvat was the central solar deity. He had a copper-colored body and rode through the sky on his chariot, which was drawn by seven ruddy horses. When he was not traveling across the heavens, Vivasvat resided in the golden city of Vivasvati. He was a nurturing deity and was often called upon for successful crops. Whenever Vivasvat was unhappy, he created the oppressive heat that caused the fields to become barren and the riverbeds to dry up.

Sanjana, Vivasvat's wife, married him despite the fact that he was made of fire and in-

tense heat. One day when Vivasvat was at his brightest, Sanjana came to him; he leaned over to kiss her, but she held up her arms and stepped away in fear—he was radiating too much heat. Vivasvat was so insulted and hurt by her response to his amorous overture that he cursed their children, Manu, Yama, and Yamuna. Manu was forced to leave the heavens and wait until the next age of men (that is, the current age), when he would become the father of humankind. Yama was banished to the underworld, where he became the king of the dead, and their daughter, Yamuna, was turned into a river.

Some tales say the Ashvins, the heavenly twins, were also Vivasvat's sons. They were the first to ride the morning sky, preceding their sister, Ushas, the dawn, and their father, the sun. The twins were bearers of medicine and could grant the gift of eternal youth.

RIGHT: Yama, god of
the infernal regions,
was feared by god and
human alike. He is
shown here in typical
fashion, mounted on
a buffalo and holding
a mace in one
hand and a noose
in another.

BELOW: This delicately
perforated Indian
shadow puppet
(depicting Hanuman
the monkey god) dates
from the nineteenth
century.

YAMA

Yama, the god of death, was the least popular of the Vedic gods. He is depicted with green skin, mounted on a buffalo. In one of his four hands he carries a mace, in another a noose.

Most importantly, Yama is the judge of the dead. According to some tales, he may have been the first man, and hence the first to die. Being the first man to reach the after-life, he founded the City of the Dead, Yamapua. Yama's sister, Yamuna, was also his wife. All inferior gods feared Yama, because they too could die.

At the gate to Yama's domain two vicious dogs, with four eyes each, guarded against any attack. Past these terrifying sentries, souls were met by Chitragupta, the registrar of the dead. He notified Yama of the soul and its mortal deeds. Yama then passed judgment on the soul, deciding whether it would be reborn, go to heaven, or enter into one of the twenty-one hells.

VAYU

Vayu, the god of storms, was often associated with Indra. Vayu alone made up the air and wind. He was without substance and at all

places at all times. Although the deer was his mount he often shared Indra's chariot as they rode through the sky. Vayu was also worshiped as the god of breath. According to legend, in a fit of rage he blew off the top of Mount Meru and hurled it into the ocean, creating what is now known as Sri Lanka.

Vayu also fathered Hanuman, the monkey god. Hanuman was the great assistant to Rama Chandra in the Ramayana. For instance, Hanuman located the captured Sita and reported her whereabouts to Rama. Hanuman was also instrumental in Sita's rescue. For all his help, Hanuman was granted eternal youth by Rama.

Although Hanuman was depicted as a monkey with human characteristics, he was capable of changing his shape and size. Being the son of the wind, he could fly. Hanuman was also known as a healer, and it was he who found the medicinal herbs that healed wounded soldiers. He was also a master of poetry and science.

VARUNA

Varuna, the god of night skies and the oceans, was responsible for the shape and brightness of the moon. Varuna helped ships find their way in the night, and it was he who put the stars in their places. Like his Greek counterpart, Poseidon, Varuna was usually depicted riding a dolphin across the ocean surface.

Varuna was also the Vedic god of honesty. He detested falsehood and generally inflicted disease, especially dropsy, upon offenders. In the Vedic pantheon Varuna was also the god of the West.

PUSHAN

Pushan, the god of nourishment, gave man cattle. Since he was a toothless god, offerings of gruel were made to him. (It was said that he insulted the great Shiva and was hit in the mouth, thereby losing his teeth.) Pushan's chariot was drawn by male goats. He was the guide for travelers and protected them on their journeys.

SOMA

Soma, the god of the moon, was also known as Chandra. He sent the morning dew. "Soma" was also the name of the ambrosia of the gods, the elixir that sustained immortality. Since the ambrosia was considered an intoxicant, Soma himself was associated with drunkenness, as was his Greek counterpart, Dionysus. He rode through the night sky in a chariot drawn by ten pure white horses. Some said the moon was inhabited by a hare and thus all hares were looked upon as incarnations of Soma.

KAMA

Kama, the god of love, was similar to the Greek Eros. He was the son of Lakshmi, the goddess of good fortune. Once Parvati sent Kama to arouse her husband, Shiva, from a deep meditation. Shiva was startled by the little god and opened his third eye. Kama was caught in the devastating beam that was emitted from the eye, and his form was destroyed. He was henceforth without physical form. His invisibility was suited to the emotion he represented, love—also a force unseen. When two people came together in union, Kama was there. He rode a wise parrot and carried a sugarcane bow with a string of bees and flower-tipped shafts.

Soma, the god of the moon (and the deity associated with an ancient rite known by the same name that involved an intoxicating drink also of the same name), rides a chariot drawn by an antelope.

THE
GODDESSES

Many sects worshiped the powerful goddesses of the Hindu pantheon. Many sects believe that these female deities were, in fact, stronger than the gods. The most often worshiped (and the most powerful) goddesses were the wives of the gods Brahma, Vishnu, and Shiva. The other goddesses, usually the wives of the Vedic gods, were not stronger but were nonetheless influential. Besides, the goddesses could ask their husbands for favors—which were rarely denied.

It is impossible to overstress the importance of the goddesses. Many sects regarded these deities as more approachable and more connected to the human experience than their male counterparts.

SHAKTI

Shakti, the mother goddess, was also commonly referred to as Sati, Parvati, Devi, Kali, and Durga. Shakti was the wife of Shiva and the goddess of wisdom. She helped guide Shiva in his sacred tasks and decisions.

As her incarnation Sati, she was the daughter of the demigod Daksha, who was Brahma's son and the personification of eternal rebirth (he died with every generation, and was reborn with each new one). Daksha was unhappy when Sati married Shiva, and slandered the god and berated his daughter. Sati could not take the incessant ridiculing, so she threw herself upon a funeral pyre. Sati's suicide was viewed as an act performed by the perfect wife, who died for her husband's honor. Without the presence of Sati, Shiva fell into a great depression and the universe became disordered.

Sati was reborn into a fishing community. She was named Parvati at birth and was fully aware, as are all incarnate gods, that her right-

ful place was in the heavens. Shiva, unaware of her birth, had a vision of his wife that instilled confidence that she would return. He resumed his meditation. Parvati tried to gain the attention of her husband, but he was too deep in thought. She prayed intensely and eventually acquired the help of Kama (the god of love). With Kama's help, she succeeded in getting his attention, and she and Shiva were reunited.

When Shiva and his wife are a single being, they are together called Devi. Devi is the male and female united in one form, representing the ideal union. Devi was the name

RIGHT: This magnificent bronze sculpture represents Devi, the unified conception of Shiva and Shakti, who are considered to have a perfect union. Understandably, Devi features both male and female characteristics. This thirteenth-century artifact is housed in the National Museum in New Delhi.

FAR RIGHT: This vibrant Punjabi watercolor depicts Durga, the warrior avatar of Shakti, slaying a demon. Typically, she is riding her lion mount and wielding several weapons. This painting is part of the collection at the Victoria and Albert Museum.

usually used in praise of the goddess. A great poem that was composed for the goddess (and some say written by the goddess) was known as "Devi-Mahatmya."

Another, fiercer incarnation of Sati was Kali. Shiva, the patron god of the demons, was usually depicted in his meditative state, calm and serene. By contrast, Shiva's wife Kali took

on characteristics of the demon, and was both fierce and vengeful. Kali was a dark and sinister incarnation. She was black as night and had a long red tongue. A truly frightening avatar, she wore a necklace of skulls and was praised as the goddess of death. Kali was capable of the same fury as the demon Rudra, the howling one.

Durga, Sati's warrior incarnation, closely associated with Kali, was known as a supreme goddess who held the universe in her womb. She radiated a yellow aura that glowed like the sun. Once when the gods were threatened by the giants Sumbha and Nisumbha, the deities turned to Shakti for help. As Durga she rode her lion into battle to protect the gods.

Shakti, of all the deities, demanded the most respect. She was the goddess of physical illusion; the goddess of life and death; the perfect wife; and a deadly warrior. Her supremacy could not be denied. Shakti was the most versatile goddess.

LAKSHMI

Lakshmi was the goddess of love, luck, and wealth. She was probably one of the most beloved of the gods because she had compassion for everyone, regardless of their caste. She could be easily flattered with praises and

gifts. When worshipers went out of their way to gain her attention, Lakshmi almost always acknowledged the supplicants by granting them their wishes.

Lakshmi, the eternal wife of Vishnu, was incarnated every time her husband was. In

FAR LEFT: This Hindu painting from 1649 is an illustration of a scene from the *Ramayana*. It shows the wedding procession from Rama's marriage to Sita, one of the incarnations of Lakshmi, goddess of love and good fortune.

LEFT: Born from a lotus, Lakshmi sits in the meditative position that takes its name from the flower.

legend, they always meet and marry. When Vishnu was reincarnated as Rama, she was reincarnated as Sita; when he was Krishna, she was Rukmini.

Lakshmi was born from a lotus flower floating on the ocean; in fact, she was brought forth from the ocean during the great churning undertaken to obtain the ambrosia of immortality. No god could deny her magnificent beauty; she was forever young and had shining gold skin laced with pearls. All the gods and demons fell in love with her, but her love was given only to Vishnu, to the despair of all the others.

Some tales portray Lakshmi as a ceaseless wanderer, roaming all lands in search of gifts and sacrifices to her. She was associated with good crops and thus good fortune. Her fellowship with the land made her the goddess of agriculture, and when one had a good crop, it was partly her doing.

Yakshini, goddess of
the woods, eighth
to tenth century,
Gyaraspur, India.

SARASVATI

Sarasvati was the goddess of learning. She was associated with the arts and sciences. As Vak, she was acknowledged as the creator of speech, including the holy Sanskrit language. All the poets and musicians praised her name, for she was responsible for giving them the fundamentals of their craft. As the wife of Brahma, Sarasvati was known as Brahmi and resided with the supreme deity in the heavenly Brahmalok.

Sarasvati—depicted as eternally young and beautiful, with four arms—had great power over her husband. When Brahma took a second wife, Brahmi (Sarasvati) was furious. Brahmi cursed Brahma as well as Vishnu, Shiva, and Indra. She said to her husband that he would fall out of man's favor, and would thus not be worshiped as widely or as often as he was accustomed. To Vishnu she said he would be reincarnated ten times. Finally, Sarasvati cursed Shiva with impotency, and foretold of Indra's defeat and the eventual loss of his kingdom.

Sarasvati favored the world of mortals and often walked among them. The mythical Sarasvati River was named for her. The swan was her favorite bird and she often rode upon an enormous swan.

OTHER IMPORTANT GODDESSES

There are many other significant goddesses in the Hindu pantheon. All of these deities seem to have direct correlations with the workings of nature. Earth itself was personified by the goddess Prithvi. She was the mother of all the gods, and was kind, loving, and gentle. Prithvi's daughter, Ushas, was the goddess of dawn as well as of poetry. Maya, the goddess of physical reality and illusion, had characteristics associated with many different gods. Maya shared her traits of versatility with the goddess Shakti. Yakshini was the playful goddess of the forest, and she frequently tried to trick travelers into losing their way. Finally, looming above the earth was the queen of the sky, Indrani. She was Indra's radiant and everlastingly happy wife.

HINDU
SERPENTS AND
DEMONS

There were two forms of serpents, the Anantas and the Nagas. Both had important roles in the functions of the universe. The Anantas, referred to as the Endless Ones, were the world serpents. They made up the mythological islands to the south of India. The Anantas also aided the gods in the churning of the ocean, at which time the universe was created and many things assumed their roles in the cosmic order.

The king of the Anantas, Shesha, was the floating island upon which the great Vishnu rested. Shesha's thousand heads sheltered the god when he slept, representing a mutual respect. Shesha's venom was very poisonous: the slightest drop from his mouth could cause mass destruction. It was believed that when one of his heads yawned, an earthquake rattled the earth.

The Nagas, closely associated with the Anantas, were also snakelike in form, but had human faces. They inhabited Patala (one of the many hells), where they answered only to Yama and Shiva. Other tales portrayed the Nagas as completely different from the Anantas; they were depicted as water deities that inhabited rivers, oceans, and lakes. It was believed that their daughters were very beautiful and often mistaken for divine humans.

ABOVE: This tenth-century carving, a detail from the Gatashrama Temple in Mathura, shows Vishnu in the meditative position. He sometimes made his home on the back of one of the Anantas.

LEFT: This seventeenth-century painting from Rajasthan is a miniature depicting Vishnu and Lakshmi riding on the back of an Ananta between two periods of cosmic evolution, destruction and creation. Many of the other deities in the Hindu pantheon are depicted, also waiting for the genesis of the new order.

The Nagas also had the duty of guarding shrines. Their forms were usually engraved in the pillars.

Demons were usually symbols of evil, or at least maliciousness. They were a nuisance to man, often causing conflict or disease. They were depicted as horrible in form, some with beastlike and some with human characteristics. The gods were involved in many conflicts with demons, and were sometimes defeated by them. Demons could be very powerful, and always had to be watched. They were ruled by Shiva, who had compassion for them

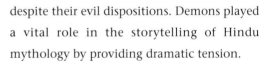

despite their evil dispositions. Demons played a vital role in the storytelling of Hindu mythology by providing dramatic tension.

There are many demons who affected man and god. The breed of Asura, the "anti-gods," were renowned for the trouble they caused the gods. The vicious Rakshasas, ruled by Ravana, were responsible for kidnapping Vishnu's wife. Ravana, who had ten heads, twenty arms, and huge fangs, was finally defeated by Vishnu's incarnation as Rama Chandra. Vishnu had been incarnated many times for the purpose of defeating demons. Another archenemy of Vishnu, Bana, had one thousand arms and was a very skillful warrior. The intervention of Shiva saved Bana from Vishnu's wrath.

The race of cannibalistic demons known as Dakini served the goddess Kali. They were savage and were often depicted with blood dripping from their mouths. Daitya, the race

of giant demons, challenged the gods many times and would have succeeded in defeating them if it hadn't been for the might of Durga, the warrior goddess.

Other demons interfered directly with the lives of mortals. The Bhuta were ghosts who misled people by mysteriously changing recognizable things in the night. It was believed that the Bhuta were once humans who died violently and consequently came to resent the living. The forest dwellers, Yakshas, also deceived men, usually by taking the form of beautiful women. Mortal men would pursue these delicious visions, but once the men had been lured deep into the forest, the Yakshas would turn into trees and leave the men lost and hopeless.

HOLY
MEN

India was the birthplace of several important religions and philosophies besides Hinduism, including Buddhism and Jainism. These belief systems are similar in that they promote self-awareness and self-betterment through specific actions. They are also similar in that each was institutionalized because of the determination of a visionary individual. Naturally, there were other important thinkers besides Buddha and Mahavira, but they were two of the most influential.

BUDDHA

Gautama Siddhartha was born in northern India in the year 566 B.C. His mother, Queen Maya of Kapilavastu, had a dream in which a white elephant floated down from the heavens on a rain cloud. The elephant circled her three times and then entered her womb on the right side of her body. Before Siddhartha was born, the sages predicted that Maya's son

would be a great holy man and not a ruler. When it was time for birth, Siddhartha emerged from Maya's right side without causing her pain. Seven days later, Maya died. When the boy took his first step, a lotus sprang where his foot touched the ground, a symbol of his holiness. Throughout Siddhartha's youth, his father sheltered him in luxury, fearful that his son would deny his royalty. At age sixteen, Siddhartha competed successfully in a contest, winning the hand of Princess Yasodhara. They had only one son, Rahula, before Gautama Siddhartha began his life's work.

On four occasions, the prince escaped the palace and explored the city. On each occasion he encountered a man whose experience was new to Siddhartha: the first was an old man, the second a sick man, the third a dead

This majestic statue of Buddha seated in a meditative stance atop a lotus flower is a fifth-century artifact that came from the northern region of India. Its discovery at a major Viking trading center in Helgo, Sweden, is a fascinating demonstration of how widespread the influence of Buddhism was.

man, and the fourth a religious man. Siddhartha was deeply moved by the human condition. As a result, he began to ponder humankind's condition. Seeing that earthly pleasures were temporal at best, he began to search for philosophical satisfaction with regard to humankind's plight. For six years Siddhartha sought enlightenment, experimenting with Brahmanic, Yogic, and ascetic religious practices.

Then in 531 B.C., the *bodhisattva* ("he who will undergo enlightenment") began to meditate under a pipal tree. Mara, the demon of death, feared that Siddhartha might achieve a state of salvation and pass on the information to humankind, ending suffering. Thus, Mara sent his seductive daughters to try to tempt the bodhisattva. Despite these diversions, Gautama remained in perfect peace and felt no sexual desire.

At the end of a period of seven days, Gautama Siddhartha had experienced his "awakening," which involved his appreciation of the Four Noble Truths. The first of these (and the kernel of Buddhist doctrine) is that all existence is suffering; the second is that the suffering has a cause; the third is that the suffering can come to an end; and the fourth is knowledge of the way in which the suffering can end. He had become Buddha, "the enlightened one."

Although Buddha had achieved the ability to look beyond his earthly self (enlightenment), he returned to the world and shared his wisdom instead of leaving his earthly form. He became a guru, teaching for forty-five years, and finally left his body at age eighty. His followers became known as Buddhists and brought his teachings to all of India. Eventually Buddhism spread to southeast Asia, where it firmly took root.

According to some Buddhist and Hindu legends, Buddha was the ninth incarnation of Vishnu (and many accounts of the sage's birth and life include references to the Vedic pantheon). The Buddhists believed that he was, in addition, one of a long line of Buddhas. The *Jataka* depicted these incarnations, of which there are 547 in all.

MAHAVIRA

Mahavira was born from semidivine means around the same time as Buddha. He was born the child of a Kshatziya family sometime in the early sixth century B.C. His mother, Trisala, after having divinely conceived, saw fourteen omens in her dreams. They were images of a white elephant, a white lion, and a white bull; the Jain goddess of good fortune, Sri; a garland of flowers; the moon and then

the sun; a golden banner and then a vase; a lotus flower floating on a lake; the expansive ocean of milk; a palace; jewelry; and finally the sanctifying fire. Trisala's husband was blessed with good fortune after the embryo appeared in his wife's womb.

As a child, Mahavira saved his friends from an attacking serpent, and this noble feat earned him his name, which means "great hero." As the young hero grew to manhood, Mahavira denounced the pleasurable life and subsequently became an ascetic. For twelve years he meditated, until, like Buddha, he reached enlightenment. He was considered the twenty-fourth (and last) in a series of both legendary and real teachers of Jainism. Each of these teachers was known as Jina, or "conqueror" (that is, of the woes of existence). Mahavira then shared his wisdom and his principles with the people, and updated and consolidated the existing Jainist doctrine. Among other things, Mahavira taught that one could escape the eternal cycle of rebirth if one achieved enlightenment.

The Jainists did not acknowledge one supreme god, but did recognize a large company of lesser deities. Like human beings, these deities were subject to the principle of *karma*, which teaches that the effect of an action will be experienced by the person who performs that action either in a current or future incarnation. The gods, subject to the same requirement as humans, had to escape the karmic cycle by living in a virtuous fashion, thereby progressing toward salvation (the release of a soul that has no further karmic obligations).

The Jains believed that Mahavira, in life, was omniscient and of divine stature. During his final sermon, when everyone went to sleep, Mahavira died in the night, unseen by his followers. He had been meditating on a throne made of diamonds when he left his body, a mere shell, behind.

This magnificent Jain temple is nestled in the hilly region of Ranakpur, located in Rajasthan, India's largest state. Rajasthan houses many of India's ancient religious sites, including Bihar, the modern name for Magadha, which was the birthplace of both Buddhism and Jainism. Mahavira was born in Magadha and spent the majority of his life preaching in and around the region.

JAPANESE MYTHOLOGY

Shinto, the "way of the gods," was the ancient native religion of Japan. A modified form of Shinto that is less a religion than a set of traditional customs is still in practice today. Shintoism emerged around 300 B.C., during a time of peace after many years of war among the clans. At this time, farming, and rice growing in particular, became the mainstay of Japanese life, so it is not surprising that in its early form, Shintoism dealt solely with agriculture. At its most basic level, Shintoism was a system of rituals and prayers for successful

Daibutsu ("great Buddha") are huge statues of the great sage, the largest of which is in Nara, near Tokyo. This daibutsu in Kamakura is over 42 feet (12.8m) high and weighs 103 tons (93t). It was rendered by Ono Goroemon, a famous sculptor of the Kamakura period.

BELOW: This thirteenth-century sculpture depicts a deity of hell holding a scroll. The Shinto underworld was believed to be a place of impurity and uncleanliness.

RIGHT: Shinto shrines, such as this one in Ise, are usually simple wooden structures that are believed to house the local *kami*, or spirits. Rituals of varying degrees of complexity, involving food, song, and dance, are performed in these shrines.

crops and, specifically, good rice harvests. Every town prayed to its own nature spirits and every family paid respect to the spirits of its ancestors. Eventually, when Japan was united under one ruling house, a common pantheon of gods was worshiped.

Like many early religions, Shintoism originated as worship of the forces of nature. Its rituals paid respect to nature for its nourishing effect and bowed to it for its destructive force. Eventually, this worship of nature evolved into a kind of pantheism, in which nature was seen to feature a host of spiritual beings, or *kami*, which controlled the elements, the terrain, the sky, and all the things below it, including the rice fields that were essential for survival.

As Shinto spread throughout the Japanese islands, it became more complex. Until the fifth century, however, when Chinese writing was introduced to Japan, the myths and practices of Shinto were transmitted orally.

The earliest text of recorded Shinto belief was the *Kojiki*, or *Record of Ancient Matters*. This text, completed in A.D. 712, upon the emperor's request, was divided into three chapters: "Life with the Gods,"

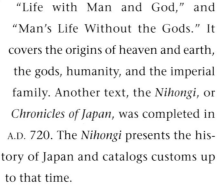

"Life with Man and God," and "Man's Life Without the Gods." It covers the origins of heaven and earth, the gods, humanity, and the imperial family. Another text, the *Nihongi*, or *Chronicles of Japan*, was completed in A.D. 720. The *Nihongi* presents the history of Japan and catalogs customs up to that time.

The *Kojiki* begins with the emergence of heaven and earth from the primeval chaos. It tells of the Heavenly Plain, where the kami first came into existence, and of the creation of the many islands of Japan.

Many of the tales told in the *Kojiki* focus on the twofold state of the spirit as being a mixture of pure and impure; one must struggle to overcome impurities in order to exist in harmony with the world. By living a pious life, humans could hope to achieve harmony with nature.

It is clear from the *Kojiki* that the kami, loosely translated as "spirit deities," were not considered gods in the Western sense. The great eighteenth-century scholar Motoori Norinaga described the kami as "anything whatsoever that was outside of the ordinary, which possessed superior power or was awe-inspiring." Thus the kami included the spirits of heaven and earth and of all the forms of nature, ancestors, nobles past and present, and, of course, the emperor and his family. Not necessarily immortal, Kami were sometimes recorded as deceased. In addition, these spirits often were believed to have mothers and fathers—indeed, entire families.

As Shintoism became more formalized, shrines were built in praise of the kami. It was believed that within each shrine, the actual essence of the kami existed; the shrines were houses for the spirits. The most important city of Shinto worship was Ise, the "Mecca" of Japan. The three shrines of Ise, said to have been built in 4 B.C., are stunning examples of shrine architecture that can still be seen today. The holy shrine of Amaterasu, the sun goddess, still houses the Sacred Mirror, one of the three treasures of the imperial regalia.

In A.D. 522, Buddhism made its way to Japan from Korea. The Korean king sent the icon of the golden image of Buddha to the Japanese Emperor Kimmei. At first, the Japanese people looked upon the idol with great doubt and suspicion. It wasn't until Chinese Buddhism (which was laced with concepts taken from both Confucianism and Taoism) was introduced that the Japanese were willing to explore its precepts. After a period of experimental worship, the golden idol was accepted by a small part of society. By the early seventh century, Emperor Shotoku introduced Buddha to all of Japan. The Japanese Buddhists, or Zen Buddhists, later honored Shotoku as a bodhisattva (a Buddha-to-be).

Buddhism, originally exported from India, changed as it developed within each new region. In Japan, the Chinese form of Buddhism converged with Shintoism to become Zen Buddhism, a very extensive system of beliefs. Shinto deities were sometimes looked upon as avatars of Buddha and protectors of sacred temples. As Buddhism became the religion of the masses, shrines were still erected in Buddhist temples to honor the Shinto spirits. In the nineteenth century, after the Imperial Restoration, the state made a vigorous effort to restore Shintoism as the religion of the nation. After Japan's defeat in World War II, however, state-supported Shinto was officially discontinued. Today, sectarian Shinto thrives as a system of traditional customs and rituals.

Following are descriptions of the more important Shinto deities who were widely worshiped before the introduction of Buddhism. This information is derived from the *Kojiki* and the *Nihongi*, as well as from popular legend.

IZANAGI
AND IZANAMI

According to the *Kojiki* and the *Nihongi*, two kami, the brother and sister Izanagi and Izanami, created the islands of Japan. They stood upon the heavenly Floating Bridge (or rainbow) and lowered the Jewelled Spear into the primeval substance below. When they re-

OPPOSITE PAGE: This slender bronze figurine of a bodhisattva was made during the Kamakura period. It is now part of the collection of the Museum of Oriental Art in Rome.

LEFT: Izanagi and Izanami, the first early spirits, stir the primeval substance to create land. The spear is called *Ame no tamaboko*, which means "celestial jewel spear."

BELOW: The Wedded Rocks at Futamigaura in Ise Bay are believed to have sheltered Izanagi and Izanami.

moved the spear, the brine dripped down off the spear's tip and formed an island. Izanagi, the "male who invites," and Izanami, the "female who invites," descended to the land, conjoined, and gave birth to the eight islands of Japan. They went on to create thirty spirits of earth, sea, seasons, winds, mountains, trees, moors, and fire. But as Her Augustness, the "female who invites," gave birth to fire, she was scorched and grew very ill.

In her sickness she gave birth to the Metal Mountain Prince and Princess, the Viscid Clay Prince and Princess, the Spirit Princess Water, and Young Wondrous Producing Spirit. Her Augustness, the mother deity, then retired from existence.

Izanagi was so stricken with grief over the loss of his sister that he wept and danced, thereby expressing his tremendous sorrow.

The strength of his emotion was such that through his grieving he created the "weeping spirit." His Augustness then sliced off the head of his son, the Fire Spirit, Kazu-tsuchi. From the blood of Kazu-tsuchi that dripped through Izanagi's fingers arose the dragon gods Kora-okami, "dragon god of the valleys," and Kura-mitsu-ha, "dark water snake." From the lifeless limbs of the Fire Spirit emerged many other spirits.

Izanagi, wishing to reunite with Izanami, descended into the "land of the night" to find her. When he came upon the entrance to the underworld, he called for his sister. Izanami came but refused to be seen. He pleaded for her to come back with him, for they had not yet finished creating the world. But she could not; she had eaten the fruit from Yami, the land of the dead. The fruit, once inside

OPPOSITE PAGE: Rice is not only a major source of sustenance to the Japanese; it is also a very important part of many rituals and customs. Because Japan has so little level land area, the Japanese developed an ingenious method of staggering rice paddies on the sides of mountains and hills.

ABOVE: The Izumo shrine, located in Matsue, is the oldest existing Shinto shrine.

Izanami, anchored her to death forever. She could never leave the realm of the dead and thus Izanami became known as the "Spirit of the Night."

His Augustness could not endure the loss, so he broke a tooth off the comb in his hair, set it aflame, and began to search for Izanami. What Izanagi found was the decaying body of Izanami. In front of his very eyes the eight thunder deities were born from Izanami's rotting flesh. His Augustness turned and fled in horror.

Shamed by her brother's actions, Izanami sent three demon spirits in the form of hags after Izanagi. When he reached the "land of the living" he threw three peaches (the divine fruit) at the pursuing hags and they retreated. Finally, Izanami herself came after Izanagi. He closed off the entrance to the underworld with an enormous boulder, then stood facing her. Izanami swore that she would each day take to death a thousand of his countrymen; Izanagi swore in return that he would cause more to be born. In this fashion, mortality came to the world.

The union of Izanagi and Izanami created the natural world; their separation caused death to come into the world. It is interesting to note that the underworld in Shinto mythology is not a place of punishment, but rather of decay and uncleanliness. Indeed, after his experience in the land of the dead, Izanagi felt the need to purify himself and immersed himself in a river.

Water, so essential to the cycle of rice farming, is a powerful symbol of purification and revitalization in Shinto belief. And as Izanagi washed, he created three of the most important Shinto deities: as he washed his left eye, the sun goddess, Amaterasu, appeared; as he washed his right eye, Tsukiyomi, the moon god and ruler of the night realm, appeared; and lastly, as he washed his nose, the storm god, Susanowo, appeared.

MAJOR
DEITIES

AMATERASU

Amaterasu, the sun goddess, is a key figure in the Shinto pantheon. (She was associated with Kunitokotachi, the supreme deity who resided atop Mount Fuji; it is even possible they may have been one and the same being.) She is also believed to be the direct ancestor of the imperial family.

The most famous story of Amaterasu tells of a falling-out between her and Susanowo, her brother. Susanowo, the storm god, had continuously bothered his sister with practical jokes and foolish behavior. When he destroyed Amaterasu's rice fields and frightened her maidens to death, she hid from him in a cave, and the radiance of the sun was withdrawn from the world. Susanowo was then banished by his father, Izanagi, and forced to rule the oceans. Meanwhile, the world grew dismal and evil spirits ran rampant.

The many earth deities, or the "spirits of the plains," assembled in front of the cave to try to coax the sun goddess out. They fashioned many gifts and offerings and began to sing and dance. Amaterasu was curious as to why the spirits were celebrating, and peeked out of her cave. A young and beautiful goddess named Uzume was dancing nearby, and Amaterasu asked the young deity why she was so joyous. Uzume said that there was now a more supreme deity than Her Augustness the Sun Goddess. When Amaterasu questioned her as to who this deity might be, Uzume presented a mirror to the sun goddess; Amaterasu then saw her own image. In the meantime, some of the other gods had proceeded in blocking the entrance to the cave. Comforted, Amaterasu returned to her throne in the heavens. The sun began to shine anew, and order returned to the world.

bloody red eyes, eight heads, eight tails, and an enormous body with a swollen belly.

Susanowo took the daughter, Kush-inada-hime, transformed her into a comb, and put her in his hair. He instructed the earth spirit and his wife to brew some sake (rice wine). He then told the earth spirit to build a fence with eight gates and eight benches, each with a vat of sake on top.

The dragon came, drank from each vat, became intoxicated, and then fell unconscious. Susanowo slew the dragon in its sleep. He then created a house in the holy city of Idzumo and married the daughter. Together they had many children.

OKUNINUSHI

Okuninushi, the "great land master," had desired Susanowo's daughter, Princess Forward, but was afraid of asking the great deity for her hand. Instead, Okuninushi tied Susanowo's hair to the ceiling beams when the god was

The first emperor of Japan, Jimmo, who ascended the throne in 660 B.C., is believed to have received the Sacred Mirror (now in the shrine of Amaterasu at Ise) directly from his divine ancestress Amaterasu.

SUSANOWO

Susanowo, the storm god and ruler of the oceans, was a trickster figure in addition to being a demon slayer. After he was banished from heaven, Susanowo descended to earth. There he came upon an old earth spirit weeping with his wife and daughter. The storm god asked why they were grieving. The earth spirit told him that a dragon arrived yearly to devour one of his daughters. When Susanowo asked what the dragon looked like, the earth spirit said it was fork-tongued with huge

RIGHT: Okuninushi
was appointed ruler
of Idzumo, one of the
holiest cities in
Japan, by his father-
in-law, Susonowo, the
storm god.

BELOW: This statue of
the Shinto deity
Nakatsu Hime Zo,
crafted during the
tenth century, can
be seen at the
Hachimangu shrine
at Nara.

asleep and secretly married the daughter. Susanowo was greatly impressed with his son-in-law's cunning and appointed him king of Idzumo, the second holiest city (next to Ise).

SUKUNA-BIKO

Sukuna-biko, the dwarf god, ruled alongside Okuninushi. He was skilled in medicine and agriculture. According to legends, he was also an incessant traveler and sailed the heavens in his boat, *Kagami*. It was believed that one day Sukuna-biko journeyed too far and disappeared into the vastness of space.

OTHER
SHINTO DEITIES

INARI

Inari, the goddess of rice, was also referred to as a "food god" (a title also given to Toyouke-hime, the supreme deity of Ise). Inari was worshiped in every Japanese farm village because she brought agricultural prosperity—

the best gift an agricultural community could hope for. When someone made a good friend or acquired some unexpected wealth, it was also Inari who was praised for her part in bringing such good fortune.

Tsukiyomi, the moon god, was invited by Inari to a huge feast that the goddess had prepared in his honor. She had laid out fields of boiled rice and bowls of fish and game. But the moon god was offended because the offerings had been spilled from Inari's mouth. Tsukiyomi destroyed the goddess and from her slain body arose crops, herds of cattle, and legions of silkworms.

HACHIMAN

Hachiman was the god of war and protector of children. His *shintai*, or "god body," was believed to be made of white stone. He was associated with agriculture, like most Shinto spirits, and was a favorite among soldiers. When Buddhism was introduced to the masses, Hachiman was looked upon as a guardian of shrines and became known as a bodhisattva.

KAGUYA-HIME

Kaguya-Hime was a celestial spirit who was at one time the most exquisite being on earth. She was abandoned when she was an infant and found by an elderly bamboo farmer. The kind farmer adopted and raised her. As Kaguya-Hime grew to womanhood, her incredible beauty became more and more impressive with each passing day. She was noticed by the emperor, who fell deeply in love with her, and they were married.

One day Kaguya-Hime revealed herself to her lord and told him that she would have to return to the heavens. He was heartbroken, but to soothe his pain she gave him a mirror that would reflect her image every time he looked into it. Then she disappeared. The emperor was so distraught that he climbed Mount Fuji, the highest point in Japan, in order to get as close as possible to his heavenly wife. But after roaming the top of the great mountain he realized he would never see her again. In a fit of lovesickness, his heart burst from his chest and smoke was sent searing into the air. Thus, the mountain became a volcano. (Fujiyama was known as the spirit of Mount Fuji. This kami was considered the guardian of all Japanese people.)

THE MIKADO

Mikado, "heavenly grandchild," was a name used to identify the emperors of Japan. The mikados were earthly, visible gods and were looked upon as spiritual leaders. The Japanese believed that they were descendants of Amaterasu, the sun goddess, and that the first mikado was actually her grandson. The heavenly kami gave the gift of grain to the mikado, who, in turn, gave it to his people for nourishment. When the mikado died, he ascended into the heavens to join the other deities.

YAMATO-TAKE

Yamato-Take was the son of the mikado Keiko, and the legendary hero of the *Kojiki*. He was a symbol of the fierce strength of nature and had attained a state of deification. Along with his fabled sword, Kusanagi, he conquered many barbarous tribes and nefarious demons.

As a boy he destroyed his brother, Opo-usu, for deceiving their father. As Yamato-Take was growing into a man, his father sent him on many missions. On one particular journey to the East, a sea deity stirred up a huge storm that sent Yamato-Take's boat drifting help-

The beauty of Kaguya-Hime, the most attractive being to appear on earth, was legendary. Her marriage to a human emperor was said to have played a part in the formation of a volcano.

This view of
Inari Sanctuary on
Honshu Island, Kyoto,
reveals the Japanese
flair for simple
architectural designs
that subtly guide
the eye and evoke
an appreciation for
line and texture.
Inari is the goddess
of rice, and thus
an important
Japanese deity.

lessly. In order to save her husband, Yamato-Take's wife sacrificed herself to the sea. On his journey home, the grieving Yamato-Take accidentally killed a god who had taken the form of a deer. This dreadful mistake doomed the young prince.

One day while climbing the mountain of Ibuke, Yamato-Take encountered a wild boar. Yamato-Take threatened that on his descent he would kill the beast. However, the wild boar was really the evil spirit of the mountain. In response to the threat, the spirit sent a severe hailstorm to pound the prince on the mountainside. Weakened by the storm, Yamato-Take eventually died. Upon his death he was transformed into a large white bird. His family chased the bird over great distances, hoping to be reunited with him, but soon Yamato-Take flew into the heavens, never to be seen again.

Dragons are among the most significant beings in Japanese lore. They are often depicted in serpentine form and can be beneficial or destructive forces.

NORTH, SOUTH, WEST, AND EAST

Bishamon, Zocho, Komoku, and Jikoku were the four Shinto spirits associated with the four cardinal directions of the compass. They were guardians of the world. Bishamon was the blue god of the north; Zocho was the white-faced warrior of the south; Komoku was the artist kami of the west; and Jikoku was the green-faced warrior of the east, who destroyed many demons.

SHINTO DRAGONS AND DEMON SPIRITS

In Shinto mythology, dragons were not always seen as creatures of destruction. They were, in fact, often looked upon as beneficial deities with great natural powers. Dragons, or *tatsu*, were often associated with water. The origins of many tatsu were told in the tale of Izanami and Izanagi, who gave birth to the Wata-tsumi, or "lords of the sea." Other dragon deities, Kora-okami and Kura-mitsu-ha, were born from the blood of the Fire Spirits, Kazu-tsuchi. Dragons were usually depicted in the form of serpents, some of whom had legs. But like the great variety of kami, dragon lore was different in each village. As water deities, the dragons were respected for their ties to the rice fields and other crops.

TENGU

Tengu were spirits, part human and part bird, that inhabited trees. They were mischievous, but not necessarily evil. They had wings on their backs, claws on their arms, and talons on their feet. They were infamous for their trickery, and their tempers would flare when tricks were performed on them.

pheasant, each of whom agreed to accompany him in return for a rice cake. Momotaro and his three companions destroyed all the demons, saved a group of imprisoned maidens, and returned the stolen treasures to the people of his village.

KAPPA

Kappa were vampire-demons who lived in water. They were small monkeylike creatures with a yellowish green hue. The tops of their heads were indented and formed basins, which contained the enchanted water that was the repository of their powers. If the demons could be tricked into bending over and spilling the water from their heads, their powers would disappear.

BUDDHISM
IN JAPAN

Until the introduction of Buddhism, Japanese religious practices lacked moral dictates and belief in an existence after death that contained reward, penance, or punishment for the actions taken in life. Shintoism was a system of prayers and offerings that in a very pragmatic way were centered on the natural cycles of agriculture and life.

Although the first icon of Buddha came to Japan from Korea, the primary teachings came from China by way of India. In China, Buddhism had already been influenced by Taoist and Confucian ideals. Chinese Buddhism—a distinctly different version from the original Indian practice—was the form that the Japanese eventually embraced. Buddhist monks traveled from China to teach in Japan; in turn, after monasteries were established, Japanese monks journeyed to China to study. The first Buddhist scripture to appear in Japan was the *Giso*, compiled by

ONI

Oni, unlike tengu, were uniformly cruel, and carried many diseases that they were more than happy to inflict on the unsuspecting traveler. Oni were human in form but had three eyes, three fingers on each hand, and three toes on each foot. They had huge mouths and devilish horns protruding from their heads. Oni were dedicated to making life unpleasant for human beings.

Momotaro, a child born from the sacred peach, was found and raised by a farming village. To thank the community for adopting and raising him, Momotaro wished to use his supernatural powers for their benefit. A nearby island had been infested with oni who often came to steal from, kidnap, and taunt the villagers. With three rice cakes to sustain him, Momotaro set out to destroy the oni. Along the way, he met a monkey, a dog, and a

Oni were malevolent spirits whose pleasure lay in causing human beings grief in the form of disease, injury, and so on. They are depicted as unsightly beings with three eyes, three fingers to a hand, three toes to a foot, and horns protruding from their skulls.

Prince Shotoku in the seventh century. One of the main Buddhist tenets explained in that text was that everything past, present, and future coexisted—that the concept of linear time was an illusion.

The Chinese developed a school of Buddhism known as *Ch'an*. In Japan, the Ch'an school became the Zen school—the most influential of the many forms of Buddhism.

Buddhism developed in Japan during four distinguishable periods. The first period was inaugurated by a great statue of Buddha erected in the Todaiji Temple at Nara, circa A.D. 752. This icon, influenced by Chinese art, made Nara the first Buddhist capital. The bronze Buddha was seated on a sacred lotus flower and measured sixty-eight feet (20.7m) in height. It was the Buddha of no time, no place, and no race, and evolved into one of the five guardian Buddhas of meditation. The Japanese praised it as the "great sun Buddha," Dainichi-nyorai.

The second period in the development of Japanese Buddhist thought occurred in Kyoto between the years 794 and 835. Dengyo Daishi and Kobo Daishi were two Japanese monks who developed a completely Japanese form of Buddhism. Kobo Daishi wrote one of the most important texts of the time, the *Ryobu*, or *Shinto with Two Faces*. He taught that Buddhism and Shintoism could coexist. One important belief introduced by the *Ryobu* was that the Shinto kami were bodhisattvas, or spiritual guardians of the Buddhist temple. Dengyo founded the Tendai sect, which later became associated with the imperial family. Dengyo and Kobo's impact lasted until the year 894, when the third period began. The sect formed by their combined teachings became known as the Shingon.

The third period came about as Japanese Buddhism matured and established uniquely Japanese traditions. This important period is

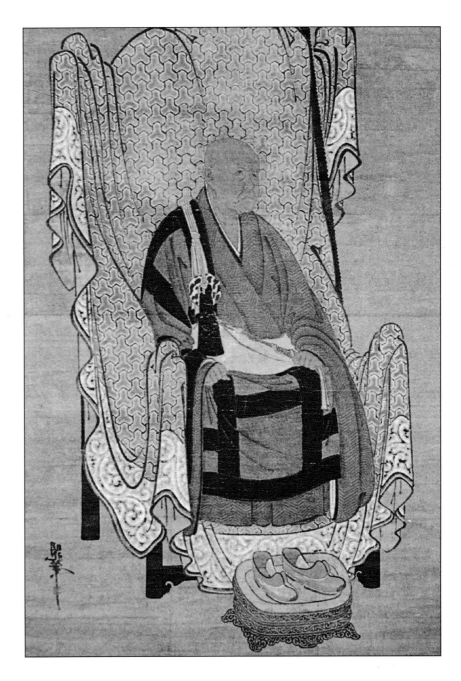

also symbolized by one of Japan's greatest works of literature, *The Tale of Genji*, written by Lady Murasaki.

The fourth period, the Kamakura, reflected the development of four distinct schools of Japanese Buddhism. They were, first and second, the Jodo and the Shinshu, which eventually converged and became known as the Amida sect. Jodo was founded by Honen and Shinran; together they taught the word and worship of the Amida Buddha as well as the seven Gods of Fortune. The third and fourth sects were Nichiren and Zen.

OPPOSITE: The Zen garden at Daitokuji Temple, Kyoto, is typically serene, featuring rocks, statuary, and coarse sand carefully raked into a soothing pattern. Zen expression is always characterized by an overriding simplicity.

ABOVE: This painting of a Zen monk highlights the characteristically simple garb worn by such men by contrasting it with a luxurious wing chair.

Nichiren, the founder of the Nichiren sect, was opposed to all other forms of Buddhism, claiming that his version alone was the only true version of Buddhism. Eisai was believed to have been the first to introduce Zen, the most influential of the sects, into Japan. (There is a Japanese saying, "The Tendai is for the royal family, the Shingon for the nobility, the Zen for the warrior classes, and the Jodo for the masses.")

Most of the mythological tales not pertaining directly to the Buddha revolve around the exploits of Japanese heroes. These legends are usually associated with the samurai and thus reflect Zen beliefs.

Zen had a significant influence on Japanese culture. This philosophy explored life from within as well as from without and bloomed in a society built on the performance of rituals. The Zen influence is felt in many important Japanese art forms: archery, swordsmanship, painting, gardening (stone gardens), ceramics, architecture (teahouses), poetry (the haiku), diet, and Noh theater. (In Noh drama, masked spirits represent demons, ghosts, or witches. They enter over a wooden bridge as if coming from another world. A single step signifies a journey. Noh drama is an exercise in the economy of gesture, movement, and symbolism. The audience experiences *yugen*, a feeling of deep contemplation of beauty.)

In the quest for enlightenment, Zen dismisses traditional patterns of thought along with the language of reason that expresses such thought. Reaching true awareness, a state of conciousness known as the "Buddha mind," requires the freeing of the mind from reason. It cannot be taught but must rather be attained, through *zazen*, "seated meditation," and the use of *koans*, mental puzzles of which perhaps the most famous is "What is the sound of one hand clapping?" Only when the mind is free of the prison of rational thought can true insight be attained. This break-

though—which takes the form of a sudden flash of insight referred to as *satori*—generally takes years to achieve, and represents the first step on the even longer road to true enlightenment.

In Japan, Zen's disciplined and practical approach appealed to members of the warrior class, the samurai. Why would something so peaceful and harmonious appeal to a warrior? The answer lies in Zen's reliance on intuition as opposed to intellect. It was only through transcending thought (*mushen*, "no mind") that one achieved enlightenment. Zen helped the warrior overcome mental restrictions in order to find the transcendent in ordinary experience. The way of the Zen warrior became known as *bushido*.

There is a story about Menechika, who was asked by Emperor Ichijo (986–1011) to forge a sword. This was a great honor and Menechika would not even think about disappointing the emperor. Menechika called upon the bodhisattva Inari, the Shinto goddess of rice, to help support his endeavor. The goddess came and whispered instructions to him, and the sword he made was magnificent. Thus, the sacred sword—two of them are worn by the samurai, with one smaller than the other—is not an object of destruction, but rather a symbol of inspiration.

ZEN HEROES
AND DEITIES

In Zen Buddhism, historical figures often attained a state of deification. This is a prime example of the historical and mythical uniting. For example, the regent Hojo Tokimune was praised as a "Buddha to be" because he defeated the invading Mongolian forces. Many tales such as this exist about Zen warriors and their accomplishments.

RIGHT: Manjusri is a warrior deity who does not destroy people—instead, he attacks their anger, avarice, and foolishness.

BELOW, RIGHT: Kwannon Bosatsu is the ultimate warrior, who moves in complete harmony with his surroundings. His ability to coordinate the movements of all of his one thousand arms simultaneously is a result of his ability to focus his mind and spirit.

Further, in the history of the faithful samurai, *ronin* appeared. A ronin was a masterless samurai who roamed the land performing honorable acts. The Zen warrior became exemplary by maintaining a pious existence.

BODHIDHARMA

The Zen belief was founded by Bodhi Dharma (Bodhidharma). Dharma was an Indian monk who traveled to China and founded the *Ch'an Tsung,* or "inner-light school," of Buddhism. In the year A.D. 520, he visited Nanking, where he presented himself to the emperor. The emperor was taken aback by this monk's cryptic way of thinking. Dharma then went on to settle in a Buddhist monastery in the north, where he spent many years in meditation. There is a tale that is told about his rigid asceticism: he once fell asleep during meditation, and when he awoke, became completely infuriated with himself. He cut off his eyelids so that he would never again pass into slumber. From his severed eyelids grew the first tea plant. Tea became the sacred drink of the Zen Buddhist.

MANJUSRI

There were Zen deities that were intimately associated with the warrior. Manjusri carried a sword in his right hand and a *sutra* (a collection of prayers) in his left. He did not kill people, but he was not merciful when it came to destroying their anger, avarice, and foolishness. Overall, he was a benevolent deity. In direct contrast to him was Acala, another samurailike god, who destroyed all those who opposed the virtues of Buddha. He was sometimes associated with the Vairocana Buddha, who was a sword himself.

KWANNON BOSATSU

Kwannon Bosatsu is depicted as having a thousand arms, with each arm holding a different weapon. Every single arm was depen-

THE DEITIES OF THE JODO SECT

AMIDA-NYORAI

Honen and Shinran taught about the "great solar Buddha," Amida-nyorai. Amida was the Buddha of "infinite light," who brought about a change in moral character. The Pure Land, Gokuraku Jodo, was where Amida resided. Gokuraku Jodo was the Buddhist heaven, or paradise; this was the place where one went upon completion of an ascetic human existence. The Pure Land is one of the most beautiful and spectacular places, filled with priceless jewels and the delightful sounds of birdsong. Amida was a compassionate and kind being who was responsible for bringing about salvation. The reward for sincere devotion to Amida was admittance into his heavenly paradise.

dent on all the others: if his mind stopped or faltered for an instant, and one hand was misused, the other 999 became useless. This is the lesson called *Prajna Immovable*, which demonstrates that one must let the mind be free. The Prajna Immovable is an attempt to attain a state of "no mind," the ability to take everything in and let everything go.

Kwannon and his mate Shoten embody the yin and yang. They are the perfect divine couple, the realization of enlightenment, an exalted state of being.

FUDO MYOO

Fudo Myoo, who was also worshiped by other Buddhist sects, was similar to Acala and was acknowledged as both the "immovable" and the "unshakable" spirit. He is depicted with sword in right hand and rope in left. His face is blazing with the threat of battle, his teeth are bared, and his eyes are glaring. He would crush all those who threatened the Buddha's teaching. He was the savior of souls and the patron of ascetics.

Early Shinto worship generally focused on objects of nature. The impressive Kinkakuji Temple, overlooking a lake in Kyoto, seems an ideal spot for such meditation, as it combines solitude and a stunning natural vista.

RIGHT: The Seven Gods of Fortune are the patrons of spiritual beneficence.

BELOW: Emmo-o was the god of death and the enemy of Amida, his polar opposite.

EMMO-O

Emmo-o, the black-faced, morbid god of death, was Amida's archenemy. He resided in his own land, which was the complete opposite of Gokuraku Jodo, the Pure Land. He was a merciless and fierce judge of the dead. Those unfortunate souls who were condemned to spend eternity in Emmo-o's domain were consoled by the gentle-faced Jizo-bosatsu. Jizo-bosatsu wandered the land of Emmo-o comforting the suffering souls. The kind and merciful Jizo-bosatsu is depicted as having a shaved head, wearing a long robe, and carrying a staff that rings when it touches the ground. It was believed that his staff had the power to ward off evil.

THE SEVEN GODS OF FORTUNE

Also associated with Honen's teachings are the Seven Gods of Fortune. These gods did not advocate physical riches or wealth, but richness of spirit.

Hotei had a huge protruding potbelly. His large belly symbolized his satisfaction, for it was filled with serenity.

Jurojin was the god of longevity. He is depicted with a long white beard and in the company of either a crane, tortoise, or deer—animals that symbolized long spiritual lives. Jurojin carried a scroll that contained the wisdom of the world.

Fukurokuju had a long, narrow head, a squat torso, and short legs. Like Jurojin, he was associated with long life and was known for his deep wisdom.

Daikoku, the patron of farmers, is often depicted sitting on a mound of rice. He carried a hammer and used it to grant special requests to favored supplicants.

Ebisu, the god of fishermen and traders, is depicted sporting a rod and his catch.

Bishamon-tenno is depicted as a powerful military monarch, clad in full armor, with spear in hand. He was prepared to battle those who opposed Buddhism. Prince Shotoku, the first of the imperial family to welcome Buddhism, called upon Bishamon to help convey Buddhist thought to the Japanese clans—noble families that were unwilling to accept Buddhism. Thus, Bishamon was a missionary as well as a warrior.

Benton was a goddess who was the bearer of wealth, patron of musicians, and guardian of speech. Benton married a sea dragon king. At first she was reluctant to marry him but after careful contemplation warmed to the idea. Their union symbolized Benton's association with the sea, and she was eventually worshiped as the goddess of the sea. Benton is often depicted riding on a serpent's, or her husband's, back. Other depictions show her playing a *biwa*, a mandolinlike instrument. She is usually found in tales about sea serpents and dragons.

OTHER JAPANESE BUDDHIST GODS

DAINICHI-NYORAI

Dainichi-nyorai, the "great sun Buddha," or "great illuminator," was associated with the Shingon sect founded by Kukai, also known as Kobo Daishi (774–835). Some say that Kukai was born with his hands clasped together in prayer. Kukai brought Dainichi-nyorai to Japan after traveling to China, where he studied *chen yen*, or "true word school." In his later years, Kukai instructed his students to bury him alive, whereupon he would wait for the coming of Miroku-bosatsu, the Buddha who has yet to come.

Dainichi is often depicted seated on a white lotus and in deep contemplation. Kukai taught that it was possible to tap into magical and spiritual powers and call upon Dainichi so that his presence could be felt on earth. It was also believed that Kukai used mystical powers—powers instilled in him by his firm belief in Dainichi—to drive away many evil dragons from Japan.

NICHIREN

Like many masters of Buddhism—including Honen, Shiron, and Eisa—Nichiren is the subject of many legends. He labeled himself a bodhisattva with "distinguished action," a protector of truth. His name means "sun lotus." Even his birth was legendary: it is said that his mother dreamed of the sun falling from a lotus flower and thus conceived Nichiren. In his teachings, Nichiren condemned all other forms of Buddhism, proclaiming his the only true one.

HAKUTAKU

Hakutaku was a strange creature who had a body resembling a hand with a human head. It was believed that Hakutaku ate humanity's bad dreams and evil experiences, freeing humans from anxiety. Hakutaku was a welcomed guest in most homes. When a family member was sick, a picture of Hakutaku was placed in the entrance of the infected person's room.

FUGEN-BOSATSU

Fugen-bosatsu is the final Buddha who has yet to come. He is the Buddha with "divine compassion" for all men. He now spreads his enlightening wisdom throughout the people. Fugen-bosatsu is depicted as a young man sitting atop a white elephant with six tusks; when he is not carrying a lotus flower, his hands are shown clasped together in prayer.

CHAPTER

III

CHINESE MYTHOLOGY

China is an ancient land of many myths and legends. The two major belief systems based on original Chinese thought are Confucianism and Taoism, which were founded by Confucius, or Kung Fu-tzu (c. 551–479? B.C.), and Lao Tzu (604 B.C.), respectively. The other important doctrine, Buddhism, was introduced into China during the Han dynasty, around A.D. 67, by traders traveling the Silk Road from India to China. With its remarkable ability to absorb and integrate outside influences, Chinese society was able to sup-

This seventeenth-century painting depicts events in the lives of certain Tang dynasty emperors. The Tang dynasty ruled for almost three centuries. In that time China experienced rapid cultural and territorial growth, with great advances in artistic output, especially in sculpture, painting, and poetry.

77

port all three schools, which shared some basic thought and eventually combined to give rise to a number of unique practices and traditions. Thus, the ancient spirits and gods coexisted with the ethical imperatives of Confucianism, the universal power of the Tao, and the meditative search for enlightenment of Zen Buddhism. Indeed, it is often noted that the Chinese follow Confucius in public life, Lao Tzu in private life, Buddha at the end of life, and the ancient traditions in daily life.

Well before these philosophies took hold, however, the people of China practiced a primitive form of worship. An early Chinese culture, the Shang people, built a complex society at the basin of the great Yellow River during the twelfth century B.C. The practices of this and earlier Chinese cultures were thought to be shamanistic, and like many such cultures often featured a belief in spirit powers, which were appeased with magic and ritual. A shaman, a respected person who could com-

municate with the spirit world, would call for rain by dancing a furious rain dance. As the shaman danced, sweat fell from his body, symbolizing the coming of rain. The shaman was also the medicine man, who healed the sick with certain potions and herbs. (These ancient herbal remedies formed the basis of traditional Chinese medicine, which still uses herbs in a holistic approach to health that has received significant attention from the Western medical establishment in recent years.) The reign of the shamanistic leader waned with the introduction of organized religion.

One enduring concept of ancient Chinese thought is the principle of opposition—light/dark, male/female, active/passive—that is part of all life. These opposing principles balance and complement one another, creating the circle of life. This concept is known as yin-yang and is central to Chinese culture. Yang is the active, positive principle, and yin is the reactive, negative principle. Yin and yang are believed to maintain the precarious balance of the universe, existing together and creating harmony. If one principle were to operate independently from the other, chaos would prevail.

The ancient Chinese traced their history from the creation of the world straight through the earliest emperors and the building of the Chinese empire with no significant distinction between the historical and the mythical. There are many periods in the development of this great culture, the histories of which are recounted through symbolic tales. The earliest ages are depicted as follows:

The earliest humans lived in trees to avoid the predatory hazards that prevailed on the ground. Then there was the period of the fire drillers, when sages first introduced fire to man so that he could cook his food—the raw food was destroying his stomach. Finally, in the earliest period of man, there were great floods; tales recount how Kung Kung, the god of water, banged his head on a mountain and tilted the earth.

Next was the period of highest virtue. During this era Jung Ch'eng, the creator of the calendar, and Chu Jung, the god of fire, came into existence.

There followed the period of the Great Ten Legendary Rulers. Fu Hsi was the first ruler and the creator of the written symbols upon which the I Ching, *or* Book of Changes, *was based. The great Yu, the champion of the great flood and founder of the Hsia dynasty, was the last.*

This magnificent Buddhist statue is from the Hsiangkuo monastery in Kaifeng, a city that has been the center of Chinese culture at several different times over the centuries. Founded in the third century B.C., Kaifeng was the capital of the Five Dynasties (A.D. 906–959) and the Sung dynasty (A.D. 960–1127).

Most of the great Chinese emperors gained deification. When an emperor died, he was buried with all his belongings: jewels, chariots, servants, and so on. Many great sages were also worshiped as gods. The most revered of these teachers were Confucius, Lao Tzu, and Bodhidharma.

The writings of most of the great sages have been permanently lost. During the Ch'in dynasty (221–206 B.C.) the Great Wall of China was built to keep the empire safe from invading forces. In contradistinction to the humanistic spirit of this architectural feat was the Burning of the Books: almost all the literature of the Ch'in and earlier eras was destroyed. Included among the burned books may have been most of the written works of Confucius. Shih Huang-Ti was the emperor whose intent was to erase the entire history of China so as to assert himself as the first em-

peror. Scholars caught meeting secretly to discuss the written word—as well as those who outwardly protested the burning—were burned to death alongside their books. This event is the cause of the gap in China's recorded history. What we know as Confucius' lessons were retold many times by his disciples and may have lost their original meaning. A text of Confucius that did survive was the *Ch'un Ch'iu* (*The Spring and Autumn*)—the history of his hometown, Lu. It is believed that some of Lao Tzu's philosophical and moral writings—collected and called the *Tao Te Ching*—also survived this devastating event.

Perhaps the most important of the surviving ancient Chinese texts is the *I Ching*. A book of prophecy and wisdom told through brief and eloquent sayings, the *I Ching* contains eight trigrams (sets of three lines, broken and unbroken) that were believed to have

OPPOSITE: This giant Buddha is from a pagoda in Soochow; at nine stories and roughly 250 feet (76.2m), it is the tallest pagoda in China.

BELOW: This Communist guard is stationed just outside the Forbidden City, Peking (or Beijing), the former seat of the imperial government. Since its adoption in 1949 as the official political ideology of China, Communism has created many such intriguing juxtapositions of old and new, as the government has tried time and again to refashion the history of this ancient culture in Communism's image.

been copied by Fu Hsi from the back of a river creature. The trigrams are used for divination. It is believed that the *I Ching* was compiled by Wen Wang and his son Wu Wang, who later went on to establish the Chou dynasty.

Of the major Chinese practices mentioned, only Buddhism was introduced after the Burning of the Books. The followers of Buddhism had to vie for popular support and thus had to adapt their philosophy somewhat to make it more appealing to the public. Throughout the many dynasties, the emperors preferred indigenous Confucianism and Taoism to the imported Buddhism, although there were periods when the three comfortably coexisted.

Buddhism introduced to Chinese belief the concept of reincarnation and the idea of hell, a realm that was the opposite of the already accepted concept of paradise. Hell in Chinese was called *ti yu*, or "earth prison." Paradise was for *hsien*, those who attained immortality, and *shen*, those who were strictly supernatural in origin. According to legend, one attained immortality by either living a good life or drinking the elixir of life.

The various beliefs of Confucianism, Taoism, and Buddhism flourished in Chinese society from ancient times to the twentieth century, when Communism attempted to eradicate religion. Yet the re-

markable staying power of these beliefs makes it likely that they will continue to be a significant part of the fabric of Chinese cultural life long after the last Marxists have gone.

THE PHILOSOPHERS

Before recounting Chinese mythology, a brief overview of the great philosophers and their tenets follows.

LAO TZU

Born in 604 B.C., Lao Tzu predates Confucius by approximately fifty years. It is believed by some that on one occasion, he discussed philosophy with Confucius, but such an encounter may be the stuff of legend. He is depicted as a reclusive but wise man, and is often pictured riding on a buffalo. Lao Tzu's name means "old boy," or "old philosopher." Little is known of Lao Tzu's actual life, although legends abound. He apparently lived a quiet life, never preaching or promoting his thought, but rather advocating a life of harmony and simplicity by living that way himself. After his death, his many disciples spread the Taoist philosophy. They taught that there was a natural order to

Sculpture flourished during the Tang dynasty, when this gilded red sandstone sculpture of the seated Buddha was made (A.D. 713).

the world, known as Tao, the "way" of the universe. Tao incorporated both the transcendent aspect of the universe—the essence of all that is—and the material aspect—the life force present in all things. Taoists tried to live in harmony with the Tao. They advocated following the principle of *wu wei*, which literally means effortless action, born of harmony with the flow of life. To follow the Tao is to avoid all friction, to turn away from desire, and in doing so to achieve all that is needed. According to the *Tao Te Ching*, a person who follows the way:

> ...*relies on actionless activity;*
> *Puts himself in the background; but is*
> *always to the fore.*
> *Remains outside; but is always there.*
> *Is it not just because he does not strive for*
> *any personal end*
> *That all his personal ends are fulfilled?*

The great thinker Chuang Tzu (c. 369 – c. 286 B.C.) popularized the tenets of Taoism through his brilliant collection of essays and stories, the *Chuang-tze*, which emphasized living in harmony with nature as an expression of the way.

T'ai chi chuan, which combines dance, martial arts, and meditation in a program based on movements copied from nature, represents another approach to Taoism.

CONFUCIUS

Confucius (also known as Kung Futzu or Master Kung) lived from 551 to 478 B.C. He was born in the small state of Lu and was a descendant of the imperial house of Shang. His father died when he was three years old, and he was raised by his mother in very modest circumstances. At nineteen he married, became a tutor, and worked toward a political career. At fifty, after many years of teaching, he was assigned a political position with status but without authority; disgusted with the corruption of the government, he resigned. It was as a teacher that Confucius excelled, and along with his followers (about three thousand in all) he began to travel from state to state teaching his moral philosophies. After thirteen years, he returned to Lu to write *Ch'un Ch'iu* (*The Spring and Autumn*), his only known surviving text.

After Confucius' death, his followers continued to spread his philosophy, gathering his lessons, thoughts, and ideas into the collection known as the *Analects* (*Lun Yu*).

Confucius lived during a time when Chinese society was in turmoil, just prior to an era known as the Period of Warring States. Not surprisingly, Confucius was principally concerned with achieving a stable society, one in which both the individual and the government would be committed to maintaining an ethical society.

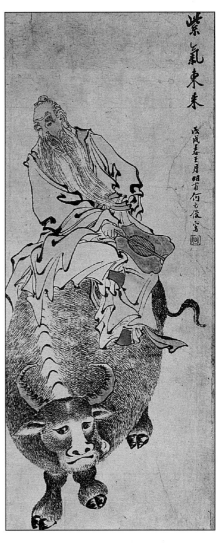

ABOVE: The influential Lao Tzu is widely depicted in Chinese art. This intricate print shows the teacher of the "way" riding his buffalo.

LEFT: This nineteenth-century engraving shows a mendicant Taoist monk and his apprentice. Such monks disseminated the tenets of Taoism in exchange for modest reward; today, Taoism is proscribed by the Chinese Communist government.

不對曰賦
与洱受以田賦詩路仲尼仲尼
不對而私語曰君子反丁
禮施取其厚事舉其中斂從其
薄若貪冒無厭則雖以田賦將
又不足文何妨焉

This early nineteenth-century scroll painting illustrates a scene from the lives of Confucius and his disciples. Above all, Confucianism is a pragmatic system of ethical precepts designed to smooth the functioning of society by providing guidelines for deportment in any of several relationships (parent and child, sovereign and subject, and so on).

Confucius' philosophy may be summed up in several concepts. The first of these, *jen*, translates as "human-heartedness," a profound respect and empathy for all people. This feeling is expressed in the Five Relationships: parent and child, elder sibling and younger sibling, husband and wife, friend and friend, and ruler and subject. Of these relationships, Confucius believed the family connections to be the most significant.

The concept of *li*, which combines propriety, or doing things the right way, with ritual, or modes of behavior, determines the conduct of these relationships.

Confucius believed that the desire to conduct oneself correctly could be instilled through example. He taught that it was therefore necessary to treat other people the way you would want to be treated.

Other important Confucian concepts include the Doctrine of the Mean, or finding the middle way between extremes, and *wen*, the importance of developing and maintaining the peaceful arts.

Ultimately, the goal of Confucianism is a society in which both individuals and the state are constantly working toward self-improvement through ethical comportment.

THE TAOIST CREATION MYTH: P'AN KU

Everything was once contained in the egg of the universe. Inside this egg slept the first living creature, P'an Ku. When P'an Ku awoke, the egg shattered. The immaculate, orderly, and light part of the egg became the sky; the unclean, heavy, and dark part became the earth. These became the forces of yin (cold earth and dark moon) and yang (bright sky and warm heaven). Fearing heaven and earth would weld together again, P'an Ku braced himself between the two forces. For the next eighteen thousand years, P'an Ku remained in this stance, growing ten feet (3m) a day, separating heaven and earth farther and farther apart.

P'an Ku also created the substance of things. His breath became the wind and clouds, and his voice created thunder and lightning. The sun came from his left eye, and

BODHIDHARMA

The legendary Bodhidharma, founder of Zen Buddhism in China, came to China from India in the year A.D. 520. It is said that he was invited by Emperor Wu of the Liang dynasty to visit Nanking. A dialogue occurred between the emperor and Bodhidharma. With each question the sovereign asked, Bodhidharma replied in true Buddhist form, with intelligent, abstract responses. Bodhidharma left the emperor's audience and settled in a monastery in the north. Here he spent the remainder of his days in meditation, staring at a wall in a Shao-lin temple.

P'an Ku, the creator and substance of the universe, plays a central role in the Taoist mythological canon. Taoism and Buddhism both adapted to existing regional belief systems by incorporating much of the supernatural into their teachings; by contrast, Confucianism— despite all its various manifestations over the ages—is essentially a secular philosophy.

the moon from his right eye. His arms, torso, and legs became north, south, east, west, and center. His blood became the rivers, and his veins roads and paths. From his flesh came the trees and soil. The hair on his head became the stars, and the hair on his body became the grass and flowers. His teeth and bones became metal and stone. His sweat became dew. Finally, the various parasites on his body became the first people.

Another variation of this myth has P'an Ku, the primeval being, chiseling the earth for eighteen thousand years. As he worked he grew six feet (1.8m) every day. The parts of his body became the substance of the earth.

P'an Ku is depicted as a dwarf wrapped in bearskin. Hammer and chisel are in hand and four sacred creatures—phoenix, dragon, tortoise, and unicorn—surround him.

NU KUA AND THE CREATION OF MAN

Nu Kua was the first creature on earth. She was half human and half dragon—from the waist up she had a magnificent womanly form and from the waist down she was serpentine. She had the magical ability to change her shape. Existence was very lonely for her, being the only creature on earth, and she began to yearn for the company of others. One day, when she was gazing into the water at her reflection, she had an idea. Scooping up some clay mud from the bottom of the pond, she began to knead and mold the clay into a little being. When she placed the character on the ground, it came to life. Overjoyed with her achievement, she made more. She worked on her creations until she was exhausted. Then she came upon another idea, and retrieved a

vine and dipped it into the wet clay. She whipped the vine around, and as the drops of clay fell to the ground they became people.

Nu Kua was proud of her achievement but realized that she could not always be responsible for creating the beings. She then divided the humans into male and female so they could reproduce on their own. She is often considered the one responsible for marriage, and is thus the goddess of marriage arrangers as well as the goddess of creativity.

Some tales link her to Fu Hsi, either as sister or consort. Fu Hsi was the first legendary first emperor of China.

The gods Kung Kung and Zhurong had decided to do battle to see who was the stronger. After many days of fighting, the great Kung Kung was defeated. He was so distressed by his loss that he rammed his horned head into Mount Pu Chou Shan. The impact caused massive destruction by fire and flood. Nu Kua's precious creations were in danger. She immediately responded by replacing parts of the damaged mount with smooth rock, and placed the legs of a slaughtered turtle at the four points on the compass to support heaven. Kung Kung's blow caused the heavens to tilt northeast, thus causing all rivers to flow east, into the ocean. Despite the destruction he caused, Kung Kung is honored in his role as a water god.

THE GREAT TEN LEGENDARY RULERS

The Great Ten Legendary Rulers of China may have been the first rulers of China as well as the historical basis for many of China's mythical beings. Their names appear again and again throughout the Chinese canon.

Fu Hsi, the first emperor, lived around 3000 B.C. He was the brother or husband of Nu Kua, the creation goddess. Often, Fu Hsi is depicted with either a fish or serpent tail. He is responsible for creating the eight trigrams upon which the *I Ching* is based.

Shen Nung was Fu Hsi's successor and ruled from 2737 to 2697 B.C. He is responsible for creating an advanced agriculture and invented the plow and a system of markets. He was the son of Princess An-teng and a celestial dragon. Fire was his element.

It was believed that his stomach was transparent, a characteristic that enabled the medicine men of the time to understand the science of gastroenterology. Early medicinal herbs were discovered by Shen Nung, and in fact, his own death may have been caused by the ingestion of a poisonous grass.

Yen Ti ruled briefly before he was overthrown by his brother, Huang Ti.

Huang Ti, the yellow emperor, began his rule in 2697 B.C. His birth was considered miraculous. In turn, he fathered twenty-five sons. At least twelve clans during the Chou period claimed to be his descendants. His rule was marked by high and low points, the lowest of which was the weakening of his senses and his subsequent inability to govern. It was during this time that he retreated to a small shack to fast and meditate. During his retreat, Huang Ti discovered the true Tao. He emerged with his strength intact and ruled the land brilliantly from then on. The development of time-telling devices, compasses, calendars, and coinage are all attributed to him.

In one depiction, Huang Ti is seen as monstrous: he has an iron head, a bronze brow, hair like swords, the body of a bull, and six arms with eight fingers each.

Huang Ti's royal procession was described like this: the wind god swept, and then the rain god dampened the road ahead. Tigers and wolves galloped first, and then Huang Ti's ivory chariot appeared. The chariot was pulled by six dragons. Spirits and serpents followed behind. Above, the phoenix flew.

Before his death, Huang Ti was taken into heaven as a *hsien* (an immortal).

This nineteenth-century engraving of Fu Hsi, the legendary first ruler of China, shows him with the eight trigrams of the *I Ching*. Fu Hsi is credited with (among other things) the creation of the first political and social system in China.

The Lungmen Grottoes (numbering around 2,100), near Loyang, contain an estimated 100,000 images of Buddha, including these colossal carvings. According to legend, the Buddhist sutras were first introduced to China in Loyang by two monks (traveling from India on a white horse) sometime in the first century A.D. Loyang was the capital of a number of ancient dynasties, including the Tang, during which period the Lungmen carvings (begun at the end of the fifth or beginning of the sixth century A.D.) were embellished.

FAR LEFT: The first of the "modern" emperors of China, Shih Huang-ti, unified the country after centuries of internecine strife in 221 B.C. Although his dynasty lasted only fifteen years, it was one of the most influential periods in Chinese history. Among other things, Shih Huang-ti created a system of roads and canals, unified the written language of China, and created the Great Wall of China. He also constructed a huge underground tomb (discovered in 1974) for himself that was peopled with an entire army of exquisitely rendered, entirely lifelike terra cotta statues, such as the ones seen here in an excavation warehouse in Xian.

LEFT: The Great Ten Legendary Rulers of China are composites of ancient history and legend.

Shao Hao ruled for only seven years. His life remains something of a mystery.

Kao Yang had eight sons, one of whom was Kun, the father of the "Great Yu."

K'u was the husband to Chiang Yuan and Chien Ti. Both of his wives were known for having conceived sons through the miraculous powers of the gods.

Yao Ti, the "Divine Yao," lived from 2357 to 2255 B.C. He was a virtuous monarch and the ultimate example of a great sage. He is responsible for employing Kun to stop the great floods, although Kun was unsuccessful; the task was eventually completed by Yu. Legend tells that the supreme god in heaven was disappointed with humanity and decided to rid the earth of man. He sent torrential rains to flood the land. Kun took pity on the people and stole some of the supreme god's enchanted soil, brought it to earth, and succeeding in damming the floods. The supreme god was angered by Kun's interference and had him destroyed. But Kun's spirit would not die. The supreme god then had Kun's limbs severed from his body. From Kun's remains, a dragon burst forth. The dragon was the Great Yu, Kun's son, who finally stopped the floods and drained the floodwaters. Yao Ti had taken an interest in a peasant boy, Shun, and offered him his two daughters to marry. Yao Ti then asked Shun to complete several tasks, one of which tested Shun's strength against the elements of fierce rain, wind, and thunder. Shun succeeded and was deemed to be strong, honorable, and pious. These distinguished qualities earned him Yao Ti's respect. Yao Ti bequeathed the throne to his son-in-law, favoring Shun over his own son.

Shun ruled from 2317 to 2208 B.C. He was a just and humane sovereign. Shun's father had remarried (after leaving his first wife) and fathered a second son. His father was a very evil and corrupt man and attempted to murder Shun. But Shun was patient with his father and never held a grudge. Shun honored his father no matter how disrespectfully the old man acted toward him. Shun is placed at the head of the Twenty-four Examples of Filial Piety (examples of great rulers who revered both their families and the governed).

Yu, the Great Yu, ruled from 2205 to 2197 B.C. Yu was the son of Kun and the grandson of Kao Yang. Kun had failed to drain the floodwaters and thus the task fell upon Yu's shoulders. For nine years Yu labored until he succeeded.

Yu was responsible for dividing China's great land into nine provinces. He also had a meeting with the ancient sovereign-sage Fu Hsi, who gave him an instrument made of jade (the sacred stone) with which he could measure heaven and earth.

Yu is depicted as having a long neck with an ugly face and a mouth like a raven's beak. He is considered the Confucian model of virtue.

YI THE GREAT ARCHER AND CHANG E THE MOON LADY

Ten suns appeared in the sky and the intense heat that radiated from them was destroying the land and drying up the riverbeds. People across the land were suffering. Yi, or Hou I, came down from heaven with his enchanted bow and shot down nine of the suns; Yi's bravery restored order over the land and sky. He later shot the celestial dog, Tien Kou, for trying to eat the moon.

Yi then set out to visit Hsi Wang Mu, the goddess of the West. Here, he obtained the precious Immortal Elixir. He was told that there was enough for his wife, Chang E, and himself. Returning home, he put it aside for the right moment and went out hunting. In the meantime, Chang E took the elixir and

started to consume it. The more she had, the lighter she felt, and she began to float into the sky. For fear that she wouldn't make it to heaven, she finished it all. Chang E kept on ascending until she reached the moon. Once on the moon, Chang E was distraught because it was barren except for the company of a certain rabbit. Yi was miserable over the loss of his wife.

Yi later took on a disciple, Peng Meng, who murdered Yi out of jealousy of his master's skill. Yi had taught Peng Meng well, and thus Peng Meng became the greatest archer alive after Yi's death.

LEGENDARY CREATURES

The dragon and the phoenix were a pair of mythical creatures that were treasured and respected by the Chinese people. Among other

OPPOSITE: The imperial history of China is so long-lived that its early history is inextricably intertwined with the country's mythological canon. A further testimony to the ritual importance with which the emperor was invested, this Tang dynasty stele (located on the summit of Taishan, in Shandong province) marks the spot where emperors performed the *feng* and *shan* sacrifices to heaven and earth, respectively. The inscription was composed by Emperor Xuan Zong when he performed the *feng* sacrifice in A.D. 726.

ABOVE, LEFT: Yi the great archer and his wife, Chang E, were a star-crossed pair.

LEFT: The phoenix, a mythical creature consumed by its own flames and reborn from its ashes as part of a regular cycle, is an emblem of royalty and was sometimes specifically associated with the empress.

a frog; the scales of a carp; the talons of an eagle; and the paws of a tiger. Dragons were believed to have been deaf. Most dragons were not winged, but had fins for swimming that were (understandably) mistaken for wings.

The scales on the dragon's body signified universal harmony. In all, the dragon had 117 scales. Eighty-one scales were under the yang influence, good fortune; and thirty-six were under the yin influence, bad fortune. The dragon was a creature of both active and reactive powers, part preserver and part eliminator.

Dragons inhabited bodies of water—the larger the body of water, the more powerful the dragon. They controlled the dispensing of rains, and created thunder by rolling huge pearls in the heavens. They were seen as both water gods and the guardians of pearls. Dragons were also the bearers of wealth and good fortune. Each town believed in its own local dragon.

The Chinese believed that there were heavenly dragons as well as earthly dragons. Those in heaven resided in the part of the sky known as the Palace of the Green Dragon. (It was given this title by the Chinese astronomers who studied the constellation of the dragon.)

Some dragons pulled the chariots of many emperors, as well as the chariot of the sun. There were also many dragon kings, known as *lung wang*, throughout China's mythological history.

This fierce warrior's head belonged to a Tang dynasty tomb guardian. His helmet is crested with a phoenix, the mythical fire bird associated with the empress. Most likely the protector of an imperial tomb, this glazed pottery figure dates from the late seventh or early eighth century.

things, the dragon represented the male characteristic, yang; and the phoenix represented the female, yin. Together these complementary creatures symbolized emperor and empress, marital harmony.

THE DRAGON

According to legend, the dragon had the head of a camel; the horns of a deer; the eyes of a demon; the ears of a cow; the long whiskers of a cat; the long neck of a snake; the belly of

THE PHOENIX

The phoenix, *feng huang*, was the sacred fire bird. It was truly a magnificent creature to behold, and it had the features of several different animals. It had the head of a swan; the throat of a swallow; the beak of a chicken; the neck of a snake; the legs of a unicorn; the arched back of a turtle; and the stripes of a dragon. Its feathers were made up of the five sacred colors: black, white, red, green, and yellow.

THE CHINESE GODDESSES

HSI WANG MU

The great Taoist philosopher Lieh-tzu tells the story of the enormous peach tree of immortality that grew on top of the highest peak in the Kwun-lun Mountains. This apex was known as the Chinese paradise. Here, Hsi Wang Mu, the goddess of the West and the empress of immortals, lived in the Jade Mountain Palace, where she tended to her magnificent gardens. Hsi Wang Mu was described as fairylike with messy hair, the teeth of a tiger, and a tail like a panther's. Sparrows—the symbol of gentleness—brought her food whenever she was out patrolling her garden. The beasts closely associated with Hsi Wang Mu were a blue stork, an albino tiger, a deer, and a huge tortoise—all gods of longevity. She also dispensed the cures for diseases.

Wu Ti, the fourth emperor of the Han dynasty, watched an uncommon-looking sparrow fly into his chamber. Tung-fang Shuo, the emperor's magician, said that the sparrow was the sign of a good omen. Indeed it was, because soon Hsi Wang Mu came to the emperor. The goddess rode in on the back of a white dragon with a procession of creatures behind her. The sight was magnificent to behold. She carried a tray with seven peaches from her immortality tree. When Hsi Wang Mu presented the peaches to Wu Ti, a few of them had been secretly eaten by Tung-fang Shuo. Wu Ti ate the remaining peaches and became immortal. (In another version of this tale, the gift was a wine elixir.)

CHUN T'I

Chun T'i is the Tao goddess of light, who radiated an enigmatic light. She had eight hands, with two holding the sun and the moon. Celestial knowledge was hers, and she rode through the heavens in her chariot drawn by seven pigs.

Chun T'i, a mythical personage in the Taoist canon, is the mother of the seven stars of the Great Bear constellation (also referred to as the Ladle), where she resides.

Dragon Hall, a pagoda in Kaifeng, China, is a magnificent example of this architectural style, which traces back to Indian Buddhism. The pagoda in all its many manifestations in Asian countries is based on the *stupa*, an ancient Indian Buddhist reliquary with a three-tiered umbrella finial.

The Chinese Buddhist version of Chun T'i was Kwan Yin, the goddess of mercy—"one who hears the cries of the world." Often Kwan Yin is depicted as a madonna with a child in her arms. Prayers of fertility were offered up to the goddess.

T'IEN HOU NIANG NIANG

T'ien Hou Niang Niang was the goddess and protector of sailors. She was closely associated with Chun T'i. The daughter of simple fishing people, one evening she had a vision of her parents trapped at sea during a storm. She ran to the beach and focused her mind on the sea. Her parents returned, the only survivors of a fleet of fishing boats that had been destroyed in a tempest. T'ien Hou Niang Niang is often called "heaven's concubine" because she is the female element of heaven.

CHIH NU

There is a popular tale of a young peasant man, Ch'ien Niu, whose only precious possession was his ox. He desired a wife and a family to fill the void in his life. Then his valued ox revealed a secret celestial identity: the ox was in fact the ox star, banished by the gods to earth for his iniquitous behavior. He offered to help Ch'ien Niu because the young man had treated him so well. The ox instructed Ch'ien Niu to go to a certain mystical spring, where at a certain time he would find the heavenly maidens bathing.

Ch'ien Niu did as he was told. He hid himself well in the bushes and waited. When the maidens came and disrobed, he grabbed the pile of clothes nearest him and made his presence known. The maidens jumped out of the water, grabbed their clothes, and flew off into the sky. The one maiden remaining cringed in terror, trying to hide her exposed body. Ch'ien Niu gave the maiden's clothes back to her. In his gesture, she felt a certain kindness and was no longer scared. He explained his situation and told her that he was seeking a wife. She accepted his proposal.

His wife was the weaving maiden, Chih Nu. They had two children, and thanks to her magical skills, the family's fortune increased. However, the gods were not in favor of their marriage and sent escorts to bring Chih Nu back to heaven. Ch'ien Niu was distraught over the loss of his wife. Again his ox intervened, telling his master that he was soon to die, and that upon his death the master should take the ox's hide and wrap himself in it. The hide was magical, and wearing it would enable Ch'ien Niu to pursue his wife. Ch'ien Niu did as instructed and then put his two children in two buckets attached to a pole. He then set off. When he was close to reaching his wife, the emperor of heaven cut a river in the sky to separate the husband and wife (this became known as the Han River, also known as the Milky Way). Ch'ien Niu's daughter asked if her father could use the ladle in her bucket to drain the river. The gods were touched by the little girl's idea and her family's efforts to reunite. In observance of the family's efforts, the gods instructed the magpies to build a bridge over the river on the seventh day of the seventh moon. On this day the family was reunited.

THE SUPREME GODS OF HEAVEN AND EARTH

The Taoists believed in a triad of gods known as the San Ch'ing, or "Three Pure Ones." The first and highest god in heaven was Yu Huang, the great jade emperor, who resided in the Jade Palace. The second god was Tao Chun, the controller of time and of the yin and yang. The third was the deified Lao Tzu, the father of Taoism.

Shang Ti was a supreme deity not associated with the heavenly triad. He was worshiped by some as the sole ruler of heaven, similar to the Western idea of one God.

On earth there were many deities who reigned. One of the most noted was Hou T'u, the prince of earth. He was a deity who in ancient times was called upon for the fertility of the soil. From his grace came all food, wood, water, and so on. In addition, every town had its own individual earth god who presided over the region and supplied people with their daily needs.

TSAO CHUN

One of the most popular gods in China was Tsao Chun, the Taoist kitchen god. A statuette of the kitchen god resided above or next to the stove in most homes. In some households today there is a poster of the deity instead of a statue. Tsao Chun is often depicted as a kind man in the company of children.

Every new year Tsao Chun leaves the household and returns to the western paradise. It is his duty to report on the behavior of the family. Each family performs a little ceremony before the god departs. A feast is offered to him, and his lips are smeared with

This nineteenth-century engraving features the minor deity Ma Chu, the goddess and protector of sailors, with two of her assistants.

RIGHT: Tsao Chun is a kitchen god of the Taoist canon. Many kitchens feature a shrine to this benevolent deity.

FAR RIGHT: This is a detail from a Ming dynasty fresco showing Kuan Ti, the spirit of war. The Ming dynasty (1368–1644) was noted for many accomplishments in the arts, particularly in the areas of porcelain making, literature and drama, and architecture.

Another popular god, who was also a historical figure, was Kuan Ti, the god of war. He was revered by Confucianists for his virtue.

When he was a young man, Kuan Ti, who was a general during the late Han dynasty, was

honey to sweeten his words. He is sometimes offered wine so that he will be in good spirits when he reports to the jade emperor.

When Tsao Chun was a man he married a beautiful woman, but fell in love with another. He left his wife and married the second woman, and soon thereafter lost his fortunes. But this was only the beginning of the unfortunate Tsao Chun's troubles. His second wife left him. He became blind and turned to the streets as a beggar. One day he happened across the house of his first wife without knowing it. She felt sorry for Tsao Chun, and fed and took care of him. The kindness was overwhelming and he began to weep. His first wife then called to him to open his eyes. When he opened his eyes his sight was suddenly restored and he recognized his first wife. In shame, he tried to escape and climbed into the fireplace. He was immediately engulfed in flames and perished.

KUAN TI

believed to have murdered a local magistrate who was molesting a girl. Fearing a reprisal for his action, Kuan Ti went into hiding. After a period of time nobody recognized him anymore, so he emerged to study and memorize many Confucian texts. Eventually, he became a god of literature.

As the god of war, Kuan Ti is often depicted as a huge, red-faced warrior with a long beard and eyes like a burning red phoenix. Both preventer and protector, Kuan Ti was not warlike by nature. However, he was always prepared to take arms against all those who attacked the empire.

PATRON GODS AND OTHER DEITIES

There were many patron gods in China who were called upon for help by persons in the many professions and trades. These deities, usually historical figures, often held jobs pertaining to their worship. Because there were so many trades, there were likewise a huge number of patron gods. Some of the more popular or more commonly invoked patron gods are discussed below.

LU PAN

The patron deity of carpenters and builders, Lu Pan is honored on the twelfth day of the sixth moon. His father was falsely accused of a crime, and in protest, Lu Pan built a huge statue of the emperor. When he finished the statue, an awful drought befell the land. The people attributed it to the statue and pleaded with Lu

Pan to do something. Honoring the people's request, he cut off a hand on the statue and the rain immediately began to fall. It was also believed that he was the creator of many tools, including the ball and socket. When a builder was stumped or needed advice, Lu Pan was always there to help.

WEN CH'ANG

Wen Ch'ang was a god of literature and patron to librarians and booksellers. As a man, he was an impoverished scholar who passed his imperial exams with the highest honors. He was to receive an award from the emperor but when the emperor gazed upon Wen Ch'ang, the award was revoked. Too ugly to be given the honor, Wen Ch'ang threw himself into the ocean in despair. But before he could drown, the ocean dragon saved him and brought him to heaven. In heaven he was made the expert of all literature. Wen Ch'ang is depicted as a small demon.

PA CH'A

Pa Ch'a, god of the grasshopper, was the protector of the crops. It was his duty to prevent pests from destroying the fields. He was depicted in human form with a bird's beak for a mouth and claws instead of feet.

T'AI SUI

T'ai Sui, the god of astronomy, historically was the minister of time. He was the son of Emperor Chou Wang.

OPPOSITE: The Wild Goose pagoda in Xian dates back to the Tang dynasty, when Xian became the western capital of China and a great center of both Buddhist and Muslim activity.

ABOVE: This flag bearer was a minor deity whose role was significant mainly to soldiers or to military mandarins.

BELOW, LEFT: This is a depiction of the goddess of midwifery seated upon a tiger; she is another minor deity, perhaps associated with Kwan Yin, the goddess of fertility.

The Great Wall of China (of which the Mu Tian Yu section is pictured here) is one of the largest and most ambitious constructions ever undertaken by human beings. Its many separate sections were unified into one wall during the reign of Shih Huang-ti and once extended for some 6,200 miles (9,920km), from the Yalu River in the northeast to Xinjiang in the northwest.

BELOW, RIGHT: Ti Yu,
a version of the
underworld, was not
an original idea of
the Chinese. The
concept came from
the Buddhists,
who also introduced
the god of the
underworld, Yama.
In China, Yama was
known as Yen-lo.

OPPOSITE: The Iren
Pagoda, located in
Kaifeng, was built
in A.D. 1049. Kaifeng
is one of the six
famous capital cities
of imperial China. In
the eleventh century,
when this pagoda was
built, Kaifeng was the
hub of the northern
Sung dynasty.

When T'ai Sui was born, he had the appearance of a shapeless blob of skin. Due to his unsightly features, associates of the emperor said he was a demon, and that both mother and child should be put to death. They were to be thrown from the palace tower, but the child was saved and was raised by Ho Hsien-ku, an immortal woman. When he was older, T'ai Sui joined the emperor's army, unbeknownst to his father. He rose to prominence in the military and then revealed himself to his father, and together they sought vengeance against those who had originally discredited T'ai Sui.

DOOR GODS

Door gods were evoked as protectors of the sick. Their likenesses were posted on both sides of a door to ward off evil spirits bent on inflicting harm.

TI YU,
EARTH PRISON

The concept of a hell—an underworld where evil spirits go after death—did not exist for the Chinese until the introduction of Buddhism. Before the idea of hell was proposed, humans sought immortality, which allowed them to reside in paradise. The introduction of the notion of hell—Ti Yu, "earth prison"—was accompanied by a new pantheon of gods. Some were directly associated with the Indian gods and some were original to China—an example of the ability of the Chinese to incorporate and expand an imported mythological canon.

The Hindu Yama, king of the underworld, became Yen-lo in China. Yen-lo's domain was not solely for evil spirits; in fact, all spirits entered through the gates of hell before proceeding to their destiny.

There were various stages that a soul had to go through. First, souls were met at the gate by demons demanding money for admission. Second, the souls were weighed on a huge scale—the good were light and the bad were heavy. Third, the souls were ushered into the Bad Dog Village, where the unblemished souls were weeded out from the corrupt souls. Fourth, they were paraded in front of the reincarnation mirror, which reflected images of their future forms. Fifth, they were brought to a terrace where they could glimpse the family they had left behind. Sixth, they were led across bridges—the evil walked over narrow bridges and the good were paraded over elaborately decorated and sturdy bridges. Seventh, they came to the wheel of law, where a drink was offered to erase all previous memories.

There were several different messengers from hell who catered to Yen-lo. Two were Mu Mien and Niu T'ou; Mu Mien had a horse's head and Niu T'ou had an ox's head. Another two were the ghostly messengers *wu-ch'ang*

kuei. Of these, the first ghost is the male, Yang Wu ch'ang, who collects those who die before the age of fifty. The other is Yin Wu-ch'ang, the female, who collects those who die after they reach fifty.

Some tales depict a deity who is even more powerful than Yen-lo. Ti-tsang Wang, or earth womb king, is the absolute ruler of the underworld. It is believed that he brought solace to those souls condemned to suffer and often delivered them from their earth prison.

P'an Kuan, the registrar of hell, is often depicted holding a book with the names of the deceased listed. His position was passed on to Chung Kuei.

SUN HOU-TZU, THE MONKEY KING

Sun Hou-tzu was born when a magical stone split in half. He was a monkey, but unlike other monkeys he had a supreme intellect and magical powers. The jade emperor of the sky took notice of Sun Hou-tzu and brought him to a special mountain where he was made king of the monkeys. After a time he decided to leave and obtain some worldly knowledge. In his journeys, Sun Hou-tzu learned how to change his form and fly. He then returned to his kingdom, only to find that it was being attacked by a demon. He defeated the demon and then turned his attention to a magical weapon that was kept by the dragon king. He approached the dragon king with such carelessness that he failed miserably in trying to obtain the magic staff.

The gods were displeased with Sun Hou-tzu's actions and wanted him to be punished. But the jade emperor was very aware of Sun Hou-tzu's aspirations to attain power and

honor, and appointed him the celestial stable keeper, an honorary post. Sun Hou-tzu thought it would bring him a nice stipend, but it didn't, and he soon left.

Sun Hou-tzu was enjoying the company of friends one day when two messengers, the wu-ch'ang kuei, approached him and tried to bring him to hell. Sun Hou-tzu was furious, for he was immortal and thus could not die, or so he said. After arguing with the messengers, he stormed off into hell. He overcame many obstacles on the way down. When he reached P'an Kuan, Sun Hou-tzu wrenched the registrar's book away and erased his name as well as those of all the monkeys he ruled.

He was now acting very arrogant and the gods began to complain bitterly. The jade emperor then made him guardian of the immortal peach tree, which belonged to the queen mother of the West. Every six thousand years the peaches on the tree ripened and the queen mother of the West held a feast for the gods. Sun Hou-tzu was so tempted by the suppleness of the fruit that he began to taste the peaches. When he found out that he was not

invited to the feast, he ate vast amounts of the peaches and drank all the wine in protest. When he had regained his senses, he was ashamed and went into hiding.

The gods had had enough of Sun Hou-tzu by this time. They found him and brought him to justice. He put up a fight the entire time, and because he was immortal—and now even more so after consuming all the peaches—the gods found it impossible to kill him. The gods finally subdued him and tied him to a stake and tried to burn him. The flames only reddened Sun Hou-tzu's eyes, and when the ropes were burned away he continued his fight.

Finally, the jade emperor called upon the great Buddha to help control Sun Hou-tzu. The Buddha presented the monkey king with a challenge: if Sun Hou-tzu could jump from Buddha's hand, then he would be made ruler of heaven. But if he could not, Sun Hou-tzu would have to return to earth. Sun accepted and proceeded to take a huge leap—a leap halfway around the world. When he had landed, he engraved his name in a rock to prove he had been there. He returned to claim his prize, but the Buddha just laughed. Sun Hou-tzu was confused; the Buddha then proceeded to show Sun Hou-tzu his palm and the place where he had engraved his name. He had never in fact left the Buddha's hand because the Buddha was everything.

Sun Hou-tzu again put up a fight, but the Buddha simply imprisoned him in a mountain for five hundred years. After this time, the monkey king had settled down. He accepted the task of accompanying Hsuan Tsang on a journey to acquire the sacred scriptures. On this journey many adventures befell the two seekers; many natural hazards barred their way; and many demons tried to destroy them.

One demon with whom they had come in contact early on in their travels was Chu

Pa-chiai, the pig fairy, also known as Pigsy. Pigsy was once a celestial character, who navigated the River Han (the Milky Way). He was banished to earth after making several lewd comments to the jade emperor's daughter. On earth, he was reborn as a pig demon and ate his family as well as other people. He was eventually converted to Buddhism, and after accompanying Hsuan Tsang on the journey to the West, was made the head altar janitor in the Western paradise.

The Great Buddha of Leshan was carved from the living rock by the monks of Leshan between A.D. 713 and 803.

BIBLIOGRAPHY

Bulfinch, Thomas. *Bulfinch's Mythology*. New York: Crown Publishers, Inc., 1979.

Campbell, Joseph. *The Hero with a Thousand Faces*. Princeton, N.J.: Princeton University Press, 1973.

———. *The Masks of God: Oriental Mythology*. New York: Viking Press, 1959.

———. *The Masks of God: Primitive Mythology*. New York: Viking Press, 1960.

Cavendish, Richard. *Legends of the World*. New York: Schocken Books, 1982.

Cotterell, Arthur. *A Dictionary of World Mythology*. New York and Oxford: Oxford University Press, 1990.

Husain, Shahrukh. *Demons, Gods, and Holy Men from Indian Myths and Legends*. New York: Schocken Books, 1987.

Knappert, Jan. *An Introduction to Oriental Mythology*. London: The Aquarian Press, 1991.

Mackenzie, Donald A. *China and Japan*. London: Bracken Books, 1992.

Morris, Ivan. *The World of the Shining Prince: Court Life in Ancient Japan*. New York: Alfred A. Knopf, 1964.

Prabhavananda, Swami, and Christopher Isherwood, trans. *Bhagavad-Gita: The Song of God*. New York and Toronto: The New American Library, 1951.

Ross, Nancy Wilson. *The World of Zen*. New York: Random House, 1960.

Sayings of Buddha. White Plains, New York: Peter Pauper Press, 1957.

Special Noh Committee. *The Noh Drama: Ten Plays from the Japanese*. Rutland, Vermont, and Tokyo: Charles E. Tuttle Company, 1985.

Suzuki, Daisetz T. *Zen and Japanese Culture*. New York: Pantheon Books Inc., 1960.

Walter, Derek. *Chinese Mythology: An Encyclopedia of Myth and Legend*. London: The Aquarian Press, 1992.

Watts, Alan. *The Two Hands of God*. New York: Collier Books, 1974.

Whitaker, Clio, contrib. ed. *An Introduction to Oriental Mythology*. Edison, N.J.: Chartwell Books, 1989.

Wilhelm, Richard, trans. *The Secret of the Golden Flower: A Chinese Book of Life*. New York and London: Harvest/HBJ, 1962.

Zimmer, Heinrich. *Myths and Symbols in Indian Art and Civilization*. New York: Pantheon Books, 1946.

INDEX